Crossing the Line

Caite Fox knows just what her boss, Jamison Wolfe, needs, even if he doesn't – or won't admit it. He's never been good at giving up control, but when passion flares between them, it becomes clear that both of them like it when she's on top.

As Caite and Jamison explore their newfound desires, each must determine the extent of their boundaries. When Caite asks something of Jamison he's not prepared to give, it seems like it's the end of them before they've had a chance to really even begin.

Can Jamison get over his fear of crossing the line, or will he lose Caite forever?

CROSSING THE LINE is a workplace, age-gap romance with *soft femdom* tropes and also grumpy vs. sunshine. The HEA is guaranteed.

CROSSING THE LINE

MEGAN HART

CROSSING THE LINE

Megan Hart

Chaos Publishing

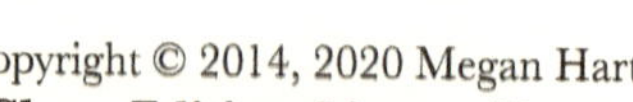

Copyright © 2014, 2020 Megan Hart
Chaos Edition, License Notes

Chaos Publishing Edition
All rights reserved.

ISBN: 978-1-951868-58-1

photo credit: DepositPhotos.com @HayDmitriy

Font credit: Showclick by www.khurasanstudio.com

cover: Chaos

Also by Megan Hart

All Fall Down

All the Lies We Tell

All the Secrets We Keep

Always You

Broken

Beg For It

By the Sea of Sand

Castle in the Sand

Clearwater

Dirty

Hold Me Close

Hurt the One You Love

Naked

Passion Model

Precious and Fragile Things

Stumble into Love

The Favor

Unforgivable

Pleasure and Purpose

No Greater Pleasure

Selfish Is the Heart

Virtue and Vice

Beautiful Thorns

Chapter One

Jamison Wolfe was shouting again.

He did that a lot. On the phone, mostly, though Caite had heard him hollering in the lobby a few times when some particularly aggressive paparazzi had managed to get past the building security and find their way to the Wolfe and Baron offices in pursuit of a few of the company's clients. Jamison lived up to his name when that happened, snarling and growling in defense of those he considered to be under his protection.

It was *totally* hot.

So far, Caite Fox had avoided being the recipient of Jamison's fury, although she'd often thought about poking him to see if she could taunt him into losing control. The thought of it had been the subject of more than a few late-night fantasies, but so far she hadn't done anything about it. First of all, teasing your boss into a hatefuck, no matter how exciting it seemed, was definitely a bad idea no matter where you worked.

Second, it was super hard to seduce a guy who barely seemed to notice you existed. Caite worked mostly with the

Baron part of the firm, Elise. Despite her constant surreptitious surveillance of her other boss, Caite usually said scarcely more than a word to him. Whenever she felt tempted to rattle his cage, instead she held her tongue and focused on staying under Jamison's rage radar, doing her work the best she could -- which was pretty damned good. She could say that and not be bragging. She'd only been with Wolfe and Baron for eight months but had already managed to accumulate an impressive client list of her own even while working on everything else her two bosses had delegated to her. This was the best job she'd ever had. Great perks, decent salary.

She considered the chance to surreptitiously ogle Jamison Wolfe one of the perks, and since he hardly gave her the time of day, she had a lot of chances to check him out without him noticing. Now the rough, deep rumble of his voice rose through the office walls and sent a shiver creeping deliciously through her, and for a moment, Caite sat back in her chair to see if she could catch a peek at him across the hall. He often paced while he hollered, and she wasn't disappointed now when he passed by his open door. Today he wore the charcoal suit with the deep pink shirt and silver and pink tie. One of Caite's favorites.

Jamison pivoted on one perfectly shined black shoe, running a hand through his dark hair and rumpling it as she watched. When he turned, the light caught the glint of silver at his temples. With the phone clamped to his ear, his brow furrowed, he looked both formidable and regal, even when he started shouting again. That was the thing about him. Unlike a lot of men who sputtered or turned red-faced and ugly in their fury, Jamison Wolfe never looked anything less than perfect.

"Caite?"

Startled, Caite swiveled in her chair to fully face the door, where her other boss, Elise Baron, had appeared. In contrast to Jamison, Elise looked anything but perfect. Her fair hair, usually pulled into a sleek French twist, had come loose around her face with pieces stuck lightly to her glistening forehead and cheeks. In the past month, her pregnancy had really begun to show, and her maternity suit wasn't as tailored or flattering as the ones she usually wore -- now her blouse had come untucked from the elastic waistband of her skirt. She'd taken off her shoes to reveal swollen feet and ankles, and her pale skin not only looked threaded with blue and red varicose veins, but also oddly dimpled, as though she'd poked a finger into rising bread dough and left behind an indentation that was only slowly filling in.

"Elise. Hey. Are you okay?"

"No. I don't think so." Elise swallowed heavily and gripped the doorframe as she swayed. "I don't feel well at all."

"Sit." Caite was up at once, taking Elise by the elbow to lead her to the futon across from her desk. Elise gave a grateful sigh as she sank onto it. "What's going on?"

"I woke up with a headache today, but I figured it was just my normal sinus stuff going on. Allergies. But it's been getting worse and I'm noticing a lot of swelling in my ankles." Elise blinked rapidly, her normally implacable demeanor shaken. "I should call Steph.”

“You sit. I’ll do it.

Of course. But I think I should call your doctor, too. You don't look good." Caite knelt in front of Elise to chafe her hands. Elise's cheeks, plump with pregnancy, nevertheless looked hollowed, her skin gray and clammy. Caite didn't know much about being pregnant beyond the fact she had no desire to get in that condition herself for a long time, but something was clearly not right. "Let me get you some water, too."

With a nod, Elise sat back against the futon's rigid cushion and closed her eyes. Caite got up and went to the water cooler in the hall, drawing a paper cup of cool water and pausing in Jamison's doorway on the way back, but he was still on the phone facing away from her. He'd moved beyond the yelling to the coldly determined, negotiating portion of the conversation, which meant he was almost finished. Poking her head around the corner to the reception area, Caite motioned to Bobby, who was busy at the front desk dealing with the mail.

"Hey. Get Steph on the line, Elise isn't feeling well. Get the number of her doctor, too. I'm going to go back and sit with her, make sure she's ok. She looked really bad."

Bobby looked surprised. "What's wrong with her?"

"Don't know. Phone, Bobby," Caite said firmly. For a guy who worked for a company that dealt in handling the media affairs of celebrities, he hadn't yet mastered the art of not being nosy.

She took the water to Elise, who didn't look any better but sipped slowly from the cup. Caite looked her over, cataloging the symptoms she could see so that when she got the doctor on the phone she'd be ready to describe them. The phone on her desk rang with the distinctive one-two beat of an internal transfer. That would be Steph, Elise's wife.

"Hey," she said, wasting no time with a greeting. "It's Caite. Elise isn't feeling well. She asked me to call you."

Steph reacted immediately. "What's wrong? Is she sick? Oh, God. Is it the baby? Is the baby coming early?"

"I don't think so." Caite quickly described the symptoms she'd noted, listening to the rapid sound of Steph's breathing. She was going to hyperventilate, at this rate. "Did you give Bobby the doctor's number?"

"Yes. Oh, God. It sounds like it's preeclampsia. I told her not to go in to work today!"

"It's going to be all right." Caite looked over at Elise, whose color was slightly better, but nothing else seemed to have changed. "Do you want to talk to her?"

Elise opened her eyes, then, and shook her head with a small smile. "Bathroom," she mouthed.

"Steph, she went to the bathroom. Listen, when...hold on, Bobby's putting a call through." Caite transferred to the other line, where she ran through the symptoms again with the doctor, who determined that it did indeed sound like Elise was suffering from preeclampsia and who told Caite she needed to be brought into the hospital immediately.

Handing the phone to Elise so she could speak with the doctor, Caite ducked back to reception, where Bobby was busy dealing with an increasingly hysterical Steph. He was good at this aspect of his job, and he handled Elise's wife with easy efficiency. Fortunately, none of them had any scheduled appointments yet this morning, and the reception waiting area was empty.

"She's going to come here," Bobby said with a hand over the mouthpiece.

"No," Caite countered. "Tell her to meet us at the hospital."

She could hear Steph's shriek of dismay all the way from across the room, but there wasn't any time to deal with that. Caite went back to rap on Jamison's door. He still had the phone pressed to his ear and gave her an irritated wave, dismissing her. Not sure how important it was to interrupt him at this point anyway -- it wasn't like the doc was calling for an ambulance or anything, right? Caite went back to her own office to find Elise on her feet. Unsteady, still pale, but looking determined.

"I need to get my stuff.

"I'll have Bobby call us a cab." Caite put out a hand to help keep Elise on her feet. "It's going to be all right."

Elise nodded, mouth wobbling as she managed to find a small, false smile. "I hope so."

Caite had no idea if everything was going to be okay or not, but one thing she was really good at was holding the hands, both literally and figuratively, of nervous people. She took Elise's hand now and squeezed. "It will be ok. You'll see."

Chapter Two

PART of the reason why Jamison liked working with Brett Dennison over at Ace Talent was that the other man knew when to stop negotiating. Not that Jamison didn't love digging down deep to figure out the right angles for the contract and getting the other guy to agree to what was best for Wolfe and Baron and nobody else. Jamison liked the power of getting someone to do what he wanted them to do...but there was also that perfect, sweet moment when the other person at last capitulated, and everything could move on from there.

"I'll have Caite work up the final agreements and send them over," Jamison said now. "Good to be working with you again, Brett."

Brett laughed. "Yeah, yeah, that's what you say when you're riding in that Beemer on my dime."

"It's not your dime," Jamison said, not bothering to point out that he did not, and never would drive a BMW. Jamison had a sixty-four Mustang that had been his old man's. Completely restored. "It's the blood, sweat and tears of your clients."

"Fair enough. Lunch next week?"

"Call Bobby. He'll set it up."

With the pleasantries out of the way, both men disconnected. Jamison sat back in his chair, finally, to put his feet up on the desk and take a breath. He'd been so caught up in his negotiation with Brett that he hadn't been paying much attention to the passing of time, but damn, the office had gone quiet. The blinking light on his desk phone told him he had messages waiting, but he didn't bother to check them. Anyone he really wanted to talk to had his cell number; anyone calling him on the office line was going to have to wait until he felt like checking in.

His stomach rumbled, and the hunger he'd been fending off since lunch, when he'd taken the time only to grab a protein bar, roared into full life. The headache followed after, poking at his temples like a dozen tiny devils dancing. With a muttered invective, Jamison pulled open his desk drawer to grab another protein bar, but the bin held only dust and disappointment.

"Dammit." He got to his feet and went to the front desk, where Bobby usually kept a basket of candy, but a few mints weren't going to do the trick.

Where the hell was everyone? Bobby might've been out the door on the dot of five, but Elise and Caite certainly should've still been finishing up some work. Elise, especially, since her plan was to get as much done as she could before she went on maternity leave. She'd planned to work from home for the first couple of months, but even so needed to get everything settled before then. Caite, on the other hand...Jamison frowned. The girl had worked in the office for all of a few months, not long enough to start slacking off, in his opinion. And dammit, there wasn't even any hot coffee in the pot Bobby was supposed to keep fresh for waiting clients. Grumbling, Jamison strode back to his office to shut everything down before he headed out.

He'd missed the ding of the elevator door opening, but looked up as the scent of pizza wafted toward him. Not pizza. Stromboli, the best kind, from Gino's down the street. He found Caite in the conference room, setting out the familiar cardboard takeout box, along with a couple of paper plates and napkins. A six pack of Troeg's Pale Ale, too. She looked up when he came in.

"Hey."

Jamison paused in the doorway. "I thought everyone was gone for the night."

Caite straightened and put a hand on one hip, her head tilting to study him for a second, lips pursed. "And you were pissed off, huh?"

"No." Well, he had been, hadn't he? At least a little. "Okay, annoyed."

She laughed, shaking her head. "You have no idea, do you?"

"About what? That everyone else around here seems to think that it's okay to skip off, whatever, just because the clock says it's time?" He frowned at her, trying to remember what they'd gone over in her initial interview, but Elise had handled most of that. "I thought we made it clear when we took you on that this wasn't going to be a nine-to-fiver."

"For your information, Mr. Wolfe," Caite said coolly, going back to setting out the food, "I was a little busy this afternoon, helping Elise."

"And that's an excuse?" The words spilled out of him, tasting irrational, and he knew it, but still a little high from his fierce negotiations with Brett, Jamison was having a little trouble coming back to the world of getting along with other people.

"You skipped lunch today, didn't you."

Jamison frowned harder. "What the hell does that have to do with anything?"

"I had to take Elise to the hospital because she was having preeclampsia, and possibly going into an early labor," Caite said, voice hard, "which you'd have known if you paid any attention to what goes on in here aside from ragging on people for not living up to your kind of asinine expectations. But if you'd eaten lunch today, I bet you'd have at least asked me what was going on before you launched into a tirade about my lack of work ethic, so sit down and eat something before *your* blood pressure gets too high."

He froze. "Elise? What? Is she all right? What the hell, why didn't someone --"

"Sit. Down," Caite commanded in a tone that sliced right through him. "Now."

Jamison sat.

They stared at each other for a moment before she pushed a plate of stromboli toward him. "Eat."

He dug in, tearing off a hunk of soft bread and gooey cheese and chewing rapidly before taking another bite. He was starving, and she was right. He was an asshole when he was hungry. But that didn't mean he didn't care about his partner.

"She's fine," Caite said before he could ask her anything else. She picked daintily at her own stromboli, cutting it neatly with her fork and knife and letting it cool before taking a bite. "They put her on some meds and are monitoring her overnight. Steph's with her. But they're not sure when she'll be back to work. Definitely not tomorrow, anyway."

"Tomorrow's the big meeting with that bunch of

yahoos from that reality show. The one about the house." Jamison reached for a beer and passed her one. He cracked the top and took a gulp, relishing the crisp flavor of the ale. "Elise was point person on that one. She knows how I feel about working with those types."

"Those types," Caite said, "are willing to pay a lot of money for our services."

Jamison paused, stromboli halfway to his mouth. He set it down. "Do I detect a note of disapproval, Ms. Fox?"

"Just truth." Caite gave him another one of those assessing looks. "They'll bring Wolfe and Baron a lot of attention, too. It's why Elise took them on. "

"And she was supposed to deal with them. I'm the guy who dots the I's and crosses the T's. She's the one who deals with the clients." After the words came out he realized he sounded unsympathetic and kind of like a dick.

Caite cracked the top off a beer for herself and tipped it toward him. "She was worried about how you'd handle it, to be honest."

"Dammit." That didn't sit well with him, not at all. "But she's going to be okay, right?"

It must've been the right thing to say, because instead of frowning, Caite gave him another slow grin. And good goddamn, that girl could smile. It lit her entire face, and Jamison couldn't understand how he'd never noticed it until just now. Maybe because this was the first time since the initial interview that he'd actually spent more than a couple minutes talking to her. It had been Elise's idea to hire her, and Jamison hadn't paid much attention beyond signing the extra paycheck.

"She'll be okay." Caite gave a firm nod, then looked hesitant for the first time tonight. "I have to believe that, anyway. Power of positive thinking."

That didn't make him feel better. "Should I call her?"

"Not tonight. Steph was going to stay with her and promised she'd call with an update in the morning. She'll be okay," Caite repeated, sounding more convinced this time. "Finish your dinner, Jamison."

He was already feeling better after having consumed just half the piece she'd given him, and he settled back in his chair with the beer. "Can we reschedule?"

"We don't have to. I'll take it on."

He sipped the beer for a moment, thinking about the new clients. He'd argued with Elise about taking them on, money or no, because if there was one thing Jamison didn't want Wolfe and Baron turning into, it was a babysitting service for douchebags. She'd fought him on it for a few reasons, money one of them. Never enough money, she'd told him, not with a baby on the way and the economy the way it was. The other reason was even simpler -- the trio of reality TV stars might be famous only for their stupidity, recklessness and lack of couth, but they were super-fucking famous. The biggest name clients Wolfe and Baron had scored to date.

"You don't have the experience," he told Caite flatly. "I'm going to have to head this one."

She sighed and rolled her eyes, not even trying to hide it. Jamison blinked, surprised both by her reaction...and his lack of it. He'd fired people for less than that. A whole bunch of them as a matter of face, which was why he and Elise and Bobby were the only ones working in this place, at least until she'd insisted on hiring Caite. But with a full belly and the beer, his favorite, mellowing him a little, all he did was grunt.

"You're going to give yourself an ulcer," Caite said.

Jamison took another long pull of beer. "You have a better idea?"

"I told you my better idea."

"You've been here, what. Six months?"

"Nearly eight," Caite said with another shake of her head that left him feeling uncomfortably ashamed.

"And you think you have what it takes?"

"I've been handling clients on my own for the past four months," Caite said quietly. "Brought some in on my own, too."

Which he ought to have known. Dammit. He'd been so caught up in his own client list that he'd been letting Elise deal with the "new hire," who, as it turned out, wasn't all that new any longer. "I thought we took you on as an assistant. Filing. Copying."

"Fetching coffee?" Caite gave him another one of those stunning grins. "Relax. I've been doing all that, too. But technically, you took me on as a junior account manager. Not an assistant."

"Elise assigned you other work, huh?" Jamison finished his beer and set the empty bottle on the table. Caite nodded. "She's a little nicer than I am."

"More than a little," came the answer.

Again, from anyone else, the smartass reaction would've probably sent him into a fury, but something about this girl...this woman, he corrected himself. Because Caite was young, but not girlish. Not at all. Something about this woman eased him away from anger. Like taking in a breath of cool air when you'd spent too long in a sauna.

"She must think highly of you," Jamison said.

"I think she's been pleased with my work. You'd be pleased, too, if you'd paid attention to it." Caite sipped her beer and gave him a long look over the top of it. "You should pay better attention, Jamison."

Something slithered through him then, at that tone.

Those words. The calmly assessing look in her blue, blue eyes. Her confidence...and that smile.

"Tell you what," he said, leaning closer. "If you can prove you can handle it, I'll let you work on this project."

"Oh, I can handle it," Caite said. "The question is, can you?"

Chapter Three

"You're a little cocky, aren't you?" Jamison said with a gleam in his dark eyes that had Caite sitting up a little straighter to meet his gaze head on.

"Pot, have you met kettle?"

To her relief, because it could've gone either way, he laughed. Then tipped his empty bottle at her before tossing it into the recycling bin next to the conference room door. "You're in for a helluva lot of work. It's not just setting up a media plan for them, you know. They're all already on all the sites --"

"I know," Caite cut in smoothly, thinking of the after-hours work she'd already put in, pulling together a media management plan for the three new clients. "It's not just monitoring their activity but doing damage control, as well as coordinating coverage when they're booked for gigs and managing that, too. Getting them sponsorships. Stuff like that. I'm not a total newbie. Before I came to work here, I had three years in social media management experience."

Jamison snorted laughter. "You probably don't remember a time when social media didn't exist."

"I'm almost thirty years old, Jamison. I can assure you, I remember a life before Connex."

He looked thoughtful. "It's not going to be easy. These kids are hard to handle."

"Which is why we got them to pay us the big bucks. Nobody else wants them, not even for the notoriety."

For a moment, she wished she hadn't said that, even though it was the truth. Wolfe and Baron were not notorious, and there was a reason for that. Jamison had started this business with an eye for clients who travelled in influential circles, but didn't make a scene. Businessmen, politicians, the occasional socialite. Once Elise had come on board, Wolfe and Baron had begun to expand into the celebrity arena, but still handled mostly theater actors, artists, classical musicians, not rock stars. Handling these three reality TV stars was totally new ground for them, but Elise had been adamant about taking them on.

Nellie Bower, Paxton France and Tommy Sanders were going to put Wolfe and Baron on the map.

And Caite intended to be part of that. She eyed Jamison now. "I can handle them."

Jamison narrowed his eyes. "What makes you think so?"

"Because I'm good at what I do. I told you. Because I think outside the box. Because I'm young and hip." She paused with a smile. "Because I've actually watched Treasure House, unlike you."

"Piece-of-shit show."

"Oh, it's a shitshow, all right, which is why it gets the ratings, and why those three are so popular right now." Caite shrugged. "Look, it's no Doctor Who, but there've been some decent episodes."

"You watch Doctor Who?"

Should she be offended at his surprise? "Um, duh. Yes."

"I used to love that show as a kid."

"Well, here's some news for you, gramps, it's been updated since then."

He looked startled at first, then gave her a grudging laugh that sent a thrill all through her. A laugh from her curmudgeonly boss was as rare as icicles in a Texas July. "Some people have lives, Ms. Fox. Like we do things other than watch television."

Somehow, she doubted that he had much of a life. It was all work with him. Hours in the office, hours outside the office. She didn't know much about his personal life, other than that he had no wife, no kids and seemingly no family. Maybe he'd sprung full grown from a trumpet, like in that old Greek myth she could never remember -- and that would make sense, because he sure had the body of a Greek god.

Hold it in girl, she counseled herself. *He's your boss and a little too bossy for you, even if he didn't sign your paycheck.*

"I have a *life*," she said instead, like a challenge.

He took it. She'd known he would. It was in the glint of his eyes and lift of his chin, and something in the way his breath shifted. She'd watched him go head to head with too many people not to know what sorts of things got him going, but had she deliberately chosen this tone of voice, those words? Caite thought that maybe she had.

"Oh, yeah?"

"Yeah," she said in a lower voice, meeting his eyes without looking away. "A rich, full life that includes time for television, along with lots of other...things."

Jamison pinned her with his gaze, his teeth bared a little in a predatory smile. "And you think I don't have a rich, full life? Why? Because I don't rot my brain with shitty reality television shows?"

"No," she said on a low breath. "Because you don't make time for those other things."

For a moment, she thought he'd reach across the table and take her by the chin. Or, oh, God, fist his fingers in her hair. But of course he didn't, and wouldn't, even if he was suddenly looking at her as though she were Little Red Riding Hood and he a different sort of wolf. Still, the look made Caite shift in her seat, squeezing her thighs together, watching him look her over.

"Like what other things," Jamison asked.

"When's the last time you went dancing, for example?"

He frowned. "I don't like to dance."

She laughed. "I'm not surprised."

For a moment, it was his turn to look offended. "What makes you say that?"

"You're not patient enough to be a good dancer."

"The hell does that mean?" His frown didn't break his face the way it would've on another man. It only emphasized his intense good looks. "Not patient enough?"

Caite shrugged. "It means that even though you're athletic and in good shape, you don't have the patience to learn any sort of coordinated dancing. And freestyle would annoy you, trying to keep up with someone who wasn't zigging left when you wanted to go right. You'd need a partner who understood you better than you know yourself, in order to keep up with you."

His mouth opened, as though he meant to speak, but Caite kept up before he could.

"You don't like crowds with loud music, and though you like to drink, you don't like being around people who are out-of-control drunk. That's why you don't like the new clients, isn't it? At least part of it?"

"They're disgusting," Jamison muttered, cutting his gaze from hers. He wiped at his mouth with his fingertips before looking back at her. "You seem to think you know an awful lot about me."

"Sorry if I overstepped," she said, not sorry at all.

Jamison wet his lips with the tip of his tongue. "You really think you can handle those three?"

"Yes. I really do." Confidence was everything; Caite had learned that a long time ago. She smiled at him, hoping to get at least the hint of a grin in return, but Jamison only stared at her steadily. For a long time.

He broke first, finally. "Fine. You're on it."

"Hooray!" Caite cried.

He looked taken aback, then shook his head and sighed. "Hooray."

"C'mon. Say it like you mean it," Caite said, standing and leaning over the table to put her hands flat on it so she could look him in the eyes. She only meant to tease him -- Jamison Wolfe had long impressed her as the sort of man who needed to be teased now and then. But at the way his eyes narrowed and mouth thinned, Caite worried she'd gone a little too far.

Then, watching him watch her, she began to hope she had.

Chapter Four

"I'll be able to call in every day." Elise, looking tired, plucked at the comforter with a surreptitious look toward the bedroom door where Steph was likely hovering. She gave Jamison a small smile. "And I'll have my laptop. I can handle some stuff from here."

"You should just take it easy." Jamison settled on the edge of the bed to pat her hand, then had a second thought and twined her fingers in his. He and Elise had been friends since high school, had spent more than a few nights tangled up in the same blankets. Never lovers, always friends, they'd shared probably every dark secret each had ever had. He knew better than anyone how unbreakable she was. And still, looking at her now, so pale and somehow shrunken despite the disconcertingly enormous mound of her belly under the blankets, all he could think about was how close he might be to losing her.

"She'll be taking it easy." Steph peeked around the doorway. "If I have to tie her to the bed, she'll be taking it easy."

"Kinky," Elise murmured with a loving smile toward

her wife that lit her eyes but didn't do much to put color back in her cheeks.

"Too much information." Jamison squeezed Elise's fingers and stood. "I'm going to head back to the office. I'm glad you're feeling better, and you take care of yourself. Stay in bed, do what the doctor tells you, you hear me?"

"Jamison, hang on. Stay a minute. Steph, baby, can you bring me some hot tea?" When the other woman had gone, Elise turned to him. "You and Caite have the new clients covered, yes?"

He hesitated, thinking about the conversation he'd had yesterday evening with the wily Ms. Fox. "She says she's good to take them over."

"You're going to have to let her. We hired her for a reason, you know."

"You're the one who told me the triplets of destruction were going to be our name makers. And you want me to leave them in the hands of our junior office assistant?"

Elise laughed. Hard. "She's a junior account manager, and she's been taking on client work since a few months after she started. Caite has a good, strong PR background, first of all. And social media savvy. Which is supposed to be our thing, you know. Remember?"

"I remember." He'd always been much better at the background aspects of the business. Getting clients and keeping them. Negotiating. Not the day-to-day handling of them, or even of the office itself. That had been Elise's expertise, and now, he guessed, Caite's.

Elise looked at him. "You can't handle everything alone, Jamison. You're going to have to let her do her job."

"And if she totally screws up? What then?"

"She won't." Elise held up a hand to keep him from saying more. "But if she does, look...those crazy kids have their own mess already. It's not like we could make anything worse for them. If anything, we should pray they screw up, big time, and soon, so we can actually work to redeem them."

"You're good at that." He laughed, thinking of a lot of the things with clients that had happened over the years. Press releases in the beginning, carefully crafted statements of apology. More recently, well-timed tweets or Connex updates.

"You need to relax." She eyed him. "You don't want to be the next one to end up in the hospital bed."

For a moment, he thought about laughing off her concern, but then he shook his head. Elise had been there with him when his dad died, too young, of a stroke and heart attack brought on by a lifetime of unhealthy habits. "I take care of myself."

"Sure. You run, you watch what you eat to the point where I wonder if you even like food. But you don't take care of yourself, honey." She paused. "I worry about you."

"You shouldn't." Her words sent a flash of heat through him. Embarrassment more than comfort. They'd been friends for a long time, and she could look right inside him, down to his core, but that didn't mean it ever felt easier to be seen that way. Jamison liked his walls high, strong, and topped with iron spikes.

"Well, you can't stop me. Now get out of here before Steph chases you out with a broom. Dinner next week?"

"Yeah. Here, I presume." He grinned, ducking away from the pillow she tossed at him. "I'll bring something good."

"You'd better." She sighed as the door creaked open and Steph appeared with a tray laden with tea and goodies. "Even though it looks like I'm going to be thoroughly spoiled as it is. Thank you, baby."

He turned away as they kissed, another tickle of heat

creeping up the back of his neck at the display of affection. It wasn't that he was...jealous, he thought as he ducked out of the room and headed for his car. Relationships were more work than they were worth. He'd had a few girl-friends over the years, and every one of them had turned out to be jealous, greedy and eventually, demanding. Even the ones who'd claimed they were only interested in some-thing casual. Which said too much about his taste in women, he admitted as he drove back toward the office. Women were a lot of work, and he wasn't the sort to be lonely, so why, then, did the memory of the sparkle in Elise's eyes when she looked at her wife leave him with such an ashen taste in his mouth?

Chapter Five

BOBBY, pushing his glasses up on his nose, looked up as Jamison got off the elevator. "Mr. Wolfe. You have several messages, and --"

As if on cue, Jamison's phone trilled from his pocket. He noted the name of the caller and sent it to voicemail. He waved at Bobby dismissively and kept going. He had stuff to take care of, first. Messages could wait.

"...And Ms. Fox is in the conference room with the clients from Treasure House," Bobby called after him.

Jamison stopped in his tracks, spinning on one heel. "Huh? They're here?"

"In the conference room," Bobby repeated, standing to point down the hall.

Like Jamison didn't know where the conference room was.

Before Jamison could sneak into his office, the conference room door opened, and Caite poked her head out. Her face lit when she saw him; the grin that spread from ear-to-ear was bright and delighted. She gestured.

"Jamison! Hi. I'm glad you're here. C'mon in and meet the Treasure House clients."

It was the last thing he wanted to do, even though meeting all their new clients was something he always did. With an inward sigh and an outwardly neutral expression, he stalked down the hall. Caite squeezed his elbow as he pushed past her.

"Deep breath," she murmured without losing a bit of her smile. "Their management is paying us triple the highest rate we're currently charging, and we've already been mentioned on three of the top five gossip sites. The phone's been ringing off the hook all day."

He glanced at her. "Since when was it triple?"

"Since I had a little talk with their manager," Caite said as her smile widened and she made a sweeping gesture to encompass the three people seated at the other end of the conference room table. "Jamison Wolfe, I'd like to introduce you to our newest members of the Wolfe and Baron family."

Here we go, Jamison thought. *The shitshow has begun.*

Chapter Six

NELLIE BOWER and Paxton France had been vociferously denying any sort of romantic relationship, but watching them canoodle on the opposite side of the conference table, Caite knew the pair were shagging like 1970s rec room carpet. Tommy Sanders didn't seem at all phased by the way Nellie reached to pluck bits of imaginary lint off of Paxton's broad shoulders, which meant he also knew the two were involved. Not that it would've been easy to ignore, since the three of them had been teamed up for the past two years, contractually obligated to be together both in and out of the house in which a multi-million dollar prize was hidden. This was the show's second season, and the stakes had risen from three to five million. If the three of them could last until the end of the season and sign on for another, the prize would rise to seven million dollars.

But it wasn't Caite's job to keep them together. Or break them up, for that matter. Her job was to spin the exploits of these three into something the public would eagerly consume, no matter how stupid they acted. Or how boring. Using her social media management skills, her task would be to keep them in the public eye without oversaturating the market, as well as making sure that everything they did met the corporate sponsors' approval.

She loved it already.

"So. Guys," she said, pinpointing her gaze on Nellie and Pax, who were ignoring her totally for a whispered conversation full of sibilance. Tommy, however, looked at her with the same deadpan stare he'd become famous for. "Let's talk about this week's schedule. You're off from the house this weekend, right?"

The team got weekends free to leave the treasure house and live in the real world while the crew reset the booby traps and clues they'd have to fight and find in the next week's filming. Pax bore a distinct set of fading bruises on his dark cheek that Caite had already seen covered in a blast of comments on the show's Connex fan page, though Pax himself had been smart enough not to breach his contract by mentioning what had caused them in anything he'd said. That had only fueled the fire of commentary as fans tried to figure out what had happened, how close to dying he'd come, the extent of injuries they couldn't see. It had been ratings genius, though Caite suspected it was mostly unplanned on his part. She was having a hard time believing Pax was smart enough to have planned that strategy.

"Yeah." The answer finally came from Tommy, who gave his teammates a small roll of his eyes. "We got the weekend off. Gotta go back in Sunday night."

"So tonight it's parrrrty!" Nellie bounced in her seat and clapped her hands like a toddler promised a pony ride. Her long black hair, dyed beneath with blue and green stripes, flipped over her shoulders. "I'ma get shit hammered!"

"There's a shocker," Tommy muttered.

From his seat, the formerly silent Jamison said, "Contractually, the three of you have to stay together at all times, right? During filming and not."

"Yeah." Pax nodded and sidled a tiny bit closer to Nellie, though it was obvious he was trying to make it look accidental. "All three of us. All the time. The three musketeers."

"More like a Payday," Tommy said.

Caite grinned at his clever twist on the names of two candy bars. "I guess it's a good thing you like each other, then."

Another one of those sly glances from Pax to Nellie. Caite didn't miss it. Jamison didn't, either. He and Caite shared a look of their own across the table.

"So," Jamison said suddenly. "Where are we going tonight?"

Chapter Seven

"YOUR FACE IS GONNA STAY that way." Caite had sidled up next to Jamison, who stood along the railing overlooking the dance floor where Nellie, Paxton and Tommy were currently taking pictures and signing autographs for their admirers. She'd arranged for the club to advertise their appearance. She didn't look at Jamison, but kept her gaze carefully on their three clients. She nudged him gently with an elbow.

He half-turned to look at her. "Don't they ever quit?"

"If you had to stay locked in a house full of booby traps, your every move being filmed, for five days out of seven...wouldn't you want to go a little wild when you had a chance for some time off?"

He shook his head. "Hell, no. I'd want to get a good night's sleep."

"You," Caite said, turning to him finally, "could stand to loosen up a little."

Jamison stared her down, but she didn't look away. "You think so, huh."

"I do."

For an instant, just the barest, briefest second, a hint of a smile ghosted along his mouth. It was gone before she could return it. But she'd seen it. There was that.

"You don't have to be here, you know. It's not required. I can handle it." Caite bounced a little on her toes to the beat of the music as she gave a discreet gesture toward their clients. She pulled out her phone to tap in an updated Connex status for the three, sending out another media blip. "We're not babysitters."

Jamison made no move to leave. "When you get them trending in the local radius, then I'll leave."

Caite's brows rose, but she held up her phone to show him the screen of her tracking app. It logged the trending topics in several of the social media apps Wolfe and Baron preferred to utilize and was updated every fifteen minutes. "We're in the top ten on most of them, except for the video ones. We had a brief surge on Buzzvid, but that was it."

"Guess you'd better get them posting some video then, huh?" He gave her a sharklike grin.

It didn't intimidate her.

"You got it," Caite said, then paused to give him a slowly quirking smile designed to get under his skin, just a little. "Boss."

She ducked through the crowd to get close to Tommy, who looked happy to see her. At least he put his arm around her and drew her close as though they were long time besties instead of just-met acquaintances. Caite didn't mind. Tommy was delicious, long and lean and tattooed. He smelled good too. He leaned close to talk into her ear.

"Hey, you."

"Can you Buzzvid a couple clips?" She looked past him to where Nellie and Paxton were holding court, happily taking pictures with fans who were hopefully using the right hashtags.

Tommy frowned for a second. "Yeah. Sure. Get in here with me."

He took a shot of the crowd, then of the two of them, with Caite woo-wooing appropriately. She waited for him to send the clip out into the world, then re-buzzed it once it had uploaded.

"You need anything? A drink or something?" Caite asked.

"Nah. I'm good. Getting tired, though. Think you can convince my compatriots over there that it's time to head home?"

She laughed ruefully, watching Nellie and Pax posing for picture after picture. Neither of them seemed tired. "Not sure about that. But you're done with this promo stuff in...five minutes. You can all do whatever you want."

He hadn't let go of her shoulders, and now half-turned toward her. "Yeah? Whatever I want?"

"Are you flirting with me?" She teased, getting ready to step out of the way so that a girl with white-blond ponytails could get him to sign her half-bared breasts.

"Only if you're interested," he said, holding up his pen with a flourish that made the blond girl squeal.

Caite had to think on that for a second or so as she looked out over the jostling crowd. There were at least a hundred girls in here tonight who'd give their right arm for a wink and smile from Tommy Sanders, much less something a little more personal. Before she could answer, he backed up a step to put an arm around her again, this time to nuzzle against her ear.

"Only if the wolf over there wouldn't bite my head off," Tommy said.

Caite followed his gaze. "Jamison? He's my boss."

"He's looking at you like he wants to gobble you up. Hey, there, what's your name?" And that was it--Tommy was back to being famous, signing boobs and posing for pictures in the last five minutes before their gig ended.

And Caite had managed to get them trending in the top five social media sites, at least for half an hour.

"Not bad," Jamison said. "Are they ready to leave yet?"

"Tommy is. Nellie and Paxton aren't. Let me guess. You are." Caite waved for a glass of ice water. The press of the crowd had left her sweating. Or maybe it had been the hint from Tommy that her boss might be interested in her. That was good for a spike in her heart rate.

"You think they're going to keep their shit together?"

Caite looked out to the dance floor, where Nellie was grinding with Pax, both of them bathed in the glare of a dozen flashes going off. Tommy joined them in a moment, bumping Nellie's ass while she shimmied. "Um. Do we care?"

"We're being paid to care."

She gave their clients another long look, then back at Jamison. "They're off the clock as of ten minutes ago. Whatever they do now is on their own time. Nellie can't go more than five minutes without posting selfies of herself. Pax, too. Tommy has a handle on what's good promo. They've been doing this for two seasons. Unless you think something's going to burn down tonight, I'd say we can leave them to their drinking and debauchery and head home."

Jamison gave her a long look. "You don't want to stay? Dance? Drink? Maybe get a little snuggly with Tommy over there?"

So. He had noticed them talking. Interesting.

Caite grinned. "He's too busy with his legions of screaming fans for the likes of lil ole me. Anyway, I just want to get home and take off these shoes and get into bed."

For a moment, she thought he might say something more, but Jamison only nodded. "Share a cab?"

"Sure thing, Boss."

"You don't have to call me that," he said when they slid into the backseat of the taxi and he'd given the driver her address.

"No?" Caite stifled a yawn with the back of her hand, glad to be out of the club's pounding beat and flashing lights. She'd done her share of clubbing in her time, and still enjoyed a night out dancing, but that place had been over-the-top crowded and too trendy for her tastes. "I thought maybe you'd like it."

"Well. I don't."

"Huh." She eyed him. "You know, in all the time I've worked for you, I don't think we've done more than share a couple words here and there."

He'd been looking out the window at the passing streets, but turned toward her now. "And?"

"Well. That's a little strange, don't you think? At the very least, bordering on unfriendly." She was teasing him a little, though there was an undercurrent of truth in her words.

"You think I'm unfriendly?" He frowned. "Since when does working with someone require you to be best friends?"

"You're best friends with Elise," she pointed out, more curious about his reaction than because she harbored any sort of long-term resentments. Up until just now, the fact that one of her two bosses pretty much left her alone had been a bonus, not a complaint.

"I've known her since high school." He looked out the window again. "You actually live in this neighborhood?"

The cab slowed to a stop in front of her building. Caite leaned forward to offer the driver her credit card, but Jamison's hand closed over her wrist and tugged it away. She glanced at him. "Yes. I do. Hey, I've got this."

"You don't." His big hand nearly engulfed hers, and his expression brooked no argument.

"I'd have billed it to the company," she said with a small grin.

Jamison didn't smile as he paid the driver. He looked again outside. "I'm walking you to your door."

Two feelings battled inside her at his words. First, the taken-aback and slightly insulted feeling of him judging her neighborhood, which, admittedly, wasn't the greatest. Especially at almost two in the morning. The second, though, was ooey gooey and spreading warm, electric tingles that started somewhere in the vicinity of her belly and quickly moved definitely lower.

"You don't have to do that, Jamison."

"I'll be fine," Caite said, but Jamison waved her to silence.

"I'm making sure you get inside. No arguing." He slid along the bench seat behind her, both of them getting out onto the cracked cobblestone pavement just down from her building. She thought she heard him mutter something about being unfriendly didn't mean he wasn't also a gentlemen.

"I never said you weren't a gentleman," Caite told him as she struggled to open her front door. The lock stuck. There was a trick to getting the key to slide in just right...

Which Jamison, apparently, had mastered, because he took the key from her hand and pushed it into the lock, then twisted, getting the door to open. It creaked, skidding along the tile floor of the entry way as it always did, because it hung unevenly on the hinges. He cringed.

"It's an old building," Caite said, hating that she felt

like she had to apologize for the wear and tear. "I like it. It's got charm."

Without asking, he followed her up the creaking, slanted stairs and into her living room. She hadn't left a light burning when she left this morning, but the pale glow coming in through the windows was enough for her to get to the switch on the wall. With the room bathed in golden light from the her dark-shaded lamps, it didn't look too bad, and she gave herself a mental kick for even daring for a second to feel as though her home was something to be ashamed of. She liked her old building with its charms and quirks.

"It looks like you," he said.

Caite thought about that for a moment, looking around to see it the way he did. "Thanks. But you really don't know me. Do you?"

"You've established that." He looked...embarrassed?

"You want something to drink?" Caite gave him a curious glance as she slung her purse onto the hooks she'd attached to the wall next to the front door and moved toward the narrow hallway leading back to the kitchen. "How about some food? I'm starving."

"I should get going," he said from behind her, but followed.

He looked too big for her tiny kitchen. Whoever had designed this apartment had been generous in carving out the living room and bedrooms from what had formerly been a single home, but the kitchen and bathroom had been given short shrift. Jamison loomed over the wee oven, the three-quarters sized fridge, the small porcelain sink. There wasn't room in there for a table, just a couple stools pushed against the bar built into the half-wall separating the kitchen from the dining room. He didn't have to hunch his shoulders to keep his head from hitting the ceiling or anything, but with those broad shoulders and long legs, he definitely filled up a lot of the space.

"I can make scrambled eggs and toast," Caite said, the words skidding around her suddenly dry throat. "Nothing's better than breakfast when you come home from the club."

He shook his head, but made no move to leave. Caite poked one of the stools toward him. He sat.

She didn't understand him. Not one bit. But instead of finding that annoying or intimidating, all it did was make her want to know him better.

The food was ready in minutes, simple eggs and sour-dough toast with real butter and jam on two pretty, delicate china plates she'd picked up at some holiday sale last year. She had orange juice, too. Coffee would've been good, but she did intend to sleep, and soon.

"Oh," she said as she slid the plates onto the bar. "And this!"

A plate of homemade scones from the authentic British bakery down the street, complete with thick, rich clotted cream. She put the plate between them and took a seat on the stool, handing Jamison a fork as she did. He took it, but absently, his attention on the phone in his hand.

"Hey. Enough. You can check the stats and stuff in the morning. Eat, now." That it already was the morning didn't escape her, but she wasn't going to point that out.

"Nellie's drunk tweeting." Jamison's mouth twisted in distaste.

"Um, that's what she does." Caite snagged his phone from his hand. "Ah, ah, ah. Be a good boy and eat your food before it's cold."

For a moment heat blazed in his eyes, and she thought he was going to lose his temper. She held his phone just out of reach, gauging if he'd grab for it. Wondering what she would do if he did.

Something grew between them.

Something thick with anticipation. Her heart thudded faster. In her fist, the phone had become heavy as a brick. Her nipples had gone tight and hard as she stared him down. Her breath caught, watching him give in to her.

Without another word, Jamison turned to his food and picked up the fork. He stabbed a bite of eggs and chewed them slowly. Silent. Caite set the phone between them on the bar, where he could easily reach it if he wanted to, and again Caite wondered if he'd take it. She would've, if it had been hers. But Jamison only ate, using the thickly buttered toast to push the eggs onto his fork.

"It's good," he said in a low voice. "Thanks. I was really hungry."

"I know you were. You didn't eat much at dinner, and if you don't eat every few hours, you get really cranky."

He paused with the fork halfway to his mouth, then set it down. "How...?"

"Look, just because you've barely given me a glance for months doesn't mean I don't pay attention to what goes on in the office." Caite nibbled her toast for a second, then washed it down with sweet orange juice. "The yelling starts right around eleven-thirty and tapers off after lunch until about three. Here. You need to have some of this, it's excellent."

She held up a scone and dripped the clotted cream all over it. But when she tried to hand it to him, Jamison shook his head. Caite waved it closer, tempting, but he wouldn't be tempted.

"I don't eat that sort of thing."

"You should," she told him, not putting it down. "Every once in a while, you need a little something sweet. Everyone does."

There it was again. That rising heat. That anticipation,

the tension between them. Caite looked into Jamison's eyes and didn't let her gaze waver, didn't put down the scone. She waited.

"No, thanks."

She put the scone on the plate and licked a few drops of cream from her fingertips, watching the way his eyes followed the motion of her tongue. Her stomach tumbled. He was her boss. This was dangerous territory. But there was no denying that something was going on here. She glanced at the phone he hadn't reached for. More heat filled her, this time centering between her thighs.

Stupid, she told herself as she leaned over the bar to tug a silk scarf from a tangle of similar accessories she'd left on the dining room sideboard. This was stupid and dangerous, and she could lose her job...She held the scarf aloft.

"You need to learn to let go sometimes, Jamison."

He eyed her warily. "You seem to think so."

It was the perfect time for him to get up and leave. Closing in on three am, stomach full, no reason for him to stay. But he didn't move.

Caite drew the silk between her fingers, enjoying the smooth fabric on her skin. "Close your eyes."

Chapter Eight

Caite waited for him to scoff. Or sneer. But he didn't. Jamison closed his eyes, and was that the slightest tremble of his lips she saw? The tiniest hitch of his breath?

Her hands shook a little when she tied the scarf around his eyes and smoothed onto his cheeks. It was an imperfect blindfold; if he tried hard enough, surely he'd be able to see. But Jamison didn't move. Standing between his legs, Caite didn't move, either.

"Open your mouth," she breathed, certain this time he'd have to deny her. He'd have to.

But he didn't. Jamison's lips parted, the hint of his tongue making her want to lean in close and taste him. She didn't, of course. Kiss her boss? Craziness, even if, dear God, he smelled so good this close that it made her knees a little weak.

Caite took a fingerful of cream from on top of the scones and let it touch the center of his lower lip. "Taste it."

His tongue crept out. A shiver ran through her. His

breath sighed out. She traced his lower lip again with the cream, this time adding a little more.

"Again."

This time, his breath shuddered out of him, and Caite put a hand on his shoulder to keep herself from having to sit. They stayed very close, neither moving. Below the blindfold, Jamison's mouth looked even more lush and inviting.

"When you can't see," she said in a low voice, "it's so much easier to give up. Isn't it?"

His hands skimmed up the sides of her thighs to settle on her hips. She didn't imagine the way his head tilted or his fingers tightened, pulling her a little closer. The heat that had been simmering between them became white hot.

Fuck this, she was going to kiss him.

His phone bleated, then buzzed against the wooden breakfast bar. Jamison's grip loosened. He pushed back from her a little, tugging at the blindfold to grab his phone. He didn't look at her as he thumbed the screen and typed in his password.

He looked at the text message, then at her. The cream had vanished from his mouth, which was good since nothing about his expression looked anything close to sweet. "Your girl Nellie just got herself arrested."

Chapter Nine

IT WAS ACTUALLY A BONUS, as far as these things went. For the company. A chance to prove that Wolfe and Baron could put a positive spin on negative situations meant that something bad had to happen, first. So it wasn't that Jamison was pissed that Caite's new clients had gotten themselves into trouble.

It wasn't that at all.

No, it was the memory of the way her fingertip had drifted over his lower lip. The taste of her mingled with the sweet clotted cream. It was knowing, deep in his gut, that her mouth would be as delicious. Her pussy even sweeter. It was thinking about how sleek the silk had been against his face, the darkness against his closed eyes. The press of his rock-hard cock inside his trousers.

All of that had put him in the worst of moods, along with the lack of sleep and having to work on a Saturday. When the call came in, Caite had calmly begun handling it in a way that had impressed him, though he wasn't willing to tell her so. Not yet. He'd been expecting to take over a bulk of the work when Elise had the baby, but now with her on extended leave, having Caite take over her clients would relieve him of a lot of work and stress...and perversely, he wasn't willing to let that all go. He'd worked too hard to build Wolfe and Baron not to cling to it. Not even if Caite Fox had her head on straight and seemed to know what she was doing. With everything.

Again, his cock throbbed as he thought of how she'd taken his phone. The way she'd known so much about him already, anticipating what he'd need or want. The simple act of making him food when he hadn't had to tell her he was hungry. Her quiet commands. Jamison closed his eyes, swallowing hard against the remembered touch of her fingertips to his lips.

"Open your mouth," she'd said, and he had, immediately. Without hesitation, responding to her steady confidence. The impression that she expected him to do as she said without question had been like putting a match to gasoline, for him. She'd said it like she owned him, and he'd let her.

That was the worst part.

"Shit," he muttered, scrubbing at his eyes. Not enough sleep and not enough coffee.

From the couch across from him, Caite stirred, and Jamison quieted. Watching her. They'd spent the past few hours putting the spin on the Nellie situation. They hadn't had to post her bail or pick her up -- her management team did that. But he and Caite had done their share of Connexing, Tweeting and posting links to positive updates about the incident, along with putting out official statements. Would it work? Time would tell, but instead of a flood of angry social media chatter about the fact Nellie had punched a girl in the face, they'd managed to at least twist the story to suggest it had been in self defense. The other girl had tossed a drink in her face, called her names. Something like that. Jamison was too tired to care.

"Morning," Caite said. She stretched like a cat, one limb at a time, and pushed her honey blond hair back from her face. She leaned forward to rub her hands on her knees. "Time izzit?"

"Just past eight."

"God. I wanted to sleep until at least nine today." She eyed him. "Did you sleep at all?"

"Some."

"In that chair?" She pointed.

Jamison nodded. Caite got up and crossed to him on bare feet. At some point during the night or early morning, as it was, she'd changed into soft pajama pants and a T-shirt. He'd declined her offer of a pair of sweats, but had conceded to loosening his tie. Now she stood in front of him, and before he could stop her, she put a fingertip beneath his chin and tilted it upward.

"You didn't sleep." She leaned, close, to look into his eyes. "You're going to be a mess."

"I'll sleep when I go home."

"Are you going home?" She hadn't moved away. Hadn't taken her fingers from beneath his chin.

His throat closed. Heart began to thud harder. He blinked, unable to look away from her.

"Jamison," Caite said slowly. "We did a good job, huh? Got things back on track, right?"

"Yes. It seems so."

"You should go to sleep." Still, neither of them moved. She studied him. "You could've left. But you didn't."

"I wanted to make sure we got this under control."

"Because you don't trust me?" she asked.

He had to admit it was true. Caite didn't seem offended. She smiled faintly.

"Because you like to be in control," she whispered. "All the time."

"I...yeah," he said, and it was the truth but felt like a lie.

"I told you, you should learn to let go a little."

This close, her eyes were wide and dark, but not brown the way he'd thought. He caught glints of gold and green. She had the faintest lines in the corners, too. She spent a lot of time smiling, then.

"I don't like--" he began.

Her hand slid from under his chin to the back of his head, where her fingers gripped his hair, tipping his face up. She wasn't hurting him, but he let out a low groan he stifled at once. She didn't laugh or even smile. If she had, he'd have been out of there before she could say a word.

"Shhh," she whispered. "Shhh."

Jamison quieted. Every muscle had gone tense, but when Caite fitted herself onto his lap, tiny tremors began to ripple through him. She cupped his face in her hands. He could not look away.

"Don't you want," she said, "to give up a little control? Just a little?"

He hadn't wanted anything so much, ever, but dammit, if that didn't piss him off even more. "Get off me."

But when she tried, his hands on her hips kept her still. They stared at each other. A breath in. A breath out. Never looking away from each other's eyes.

"You should get off," he whispered.

"Oh, I'd love to," Caite said. "I'd like to get off very much."

His cock surged at the innuendo. His fingers gripped her smooth, warm skin just above the waistband of her pajamas. The feeling of it made him want to get on his knees in front of her. To open her thighs and use his mouth on her. To hear her cry out his name as she came.

Jamison didn't move.

Caite rocked her hips the tiniest amount, pressing herself against the bulge in his pants. Her eyes never left his. "When's the last time you fucked a woman, not your hand?"

He said nothing.

"When," she said, rocking a little harder, "is the last time you came?"

It had been just over a week, but he kept his mouth closed tight. He could stand, tumbling her off his lap, but something stopped him. The look in her eyes? The sound of her voice. The way her hands felt on his face as she kept him still, forcing him to look into her eyes.

"I'm going to kiss you," Caite said softly but firmly. "Are you going to let me?"

Jamison meant to say "no," but what came out was nothing but a sigh. She tilted her head. Her lips brushed his, but she didn't kiss him. Not yet. She let her breath caress him, teasing. The weight of her on his lap was so slight it was like holding air, and yet the pressure of her body on his erection was enough to make him grunt in frustration when she rocked on him again.

His mouth opened, seeking hers, but she held him still.

"No," she said. "I told you, I'm going to kiss *you*."

He waited, heart pounding so hard he swore he could hear the thunder of it outside his chest. He counted the seconds, the breaths, the pulse of blood in his engorged prick. He thought he would tell her to get the fuck off his lap. He thought he'd turn his head to keep his mouth from hers, but in the end all he did was wait for Caite to kiss him.

She did.

And he was lost.

Chapter Ten

CAITE SLANTED her mouth to Jamison's, the press of her lips light at first but quickly getting harder as soon as he opened for her. The soft sigh of his moan against her lips sent a shiver through her, but what really got her going was the way he totally succumbed to her. She'd noticed it a few times already, his reactions to the way she took command. Every time she'd thought he would balk or outright refuse her, he had not, and he wasn't now. It set her on fire.

"You work hard," she told him now, every word brushing her mouth on his. "But you have to learn to let a few things go."

His fingers tightened on her hips, digging just hard enough promise pain if he kept going. He didn't. Caite wasn't sure if she were relieved or disappointed.

"If you want something done right, you have to make sure you do it yourself," Jamison breathed.

"Okay. Boss."

"I told you not to call me that."

Caite laughed, then paused, waiting for the subtle feeling of his body straining toward hers. When she felt it, that tension, the flex and release of his muscles and the soft caress of his breath on her mouth, she brushed his lips with hers again. She wanted to take his mouth and plunder it, fuck into it with her tongue while she pulled his hair so tight he couldn't move...except he could move, that was the thrill of it. He could toss her off his lap. Push her away. She couldn't control him, not physically, unless he let her, and oh, shit, he was letting her.

"You don't hover over Elise."

Jamison licked his lips, touching hers with his tongue. "You're not Elise."

She'd have been pissed off if she wasn't so turned on. She held his face a little tighter, tipping it up. "Thank God for that, or else you wouldn't be rock hard right now."

He did try to pull away then, but not with enough force to make her let him go. Caite ground herself against him a little harder. She meant it to tease him, but it felt so good that she shuddered. It had been months since her last relationship ended, and she hadn't had so much as a one nighter since then. Touching him, tasting him, all she could think about was feeling him inside her.

"You taste so good," she whispered into his mouth. "Open. Let me taste you more."

Surely this time he'd refuse her. Put her off his lap, stalk out the door. Hell, maybe he'd fire her for good measure. But no, Jamison's mouth opened and he gave her his tongue. His cock, thick and hard and oh, shit, yes, throbbing, pushed against her clit. She wore only a thin pair of flannel pj bottoms and no panties, and every movement rubbed her bare pussy against the soft fabric.

"That feels so good," she murmured, rocking her hips.

His hands tightened again. He kissed her harder, and she let him. Their teeth clashed. Tongues battled. His hands slid down to cup her ass, pushing her against him harder. Faster. Together they rocked so hard the chair creaked.

Her orgasm coiled tight and tighter, building. She was going to come from this--not from just the consistent, delicious pressure of her clit against him but from everything else. The way he'd given in to her. The way he shuddered now.

"Oh," she said, surprised. "Yes. Right there. Like that."

Pleasure filled her like a river rushing through a canyon. She shook with it, her hands still cupping his face. Her mouth on his. The copper taste of blood forced her eyes open -- she'd nipped his lower lip. Jamison didn't seem to care, his own eyes closed, cock still hard and pushing against her. When she quieted, sighing his name, he opened his eyes.

Something nameless twisted between them.

Caite swallowed, licking her lips of the last taste of him. She drew in a breath, blinking to clear her head. With someone else she'd be reaching between them to unzip him, to get her hands on him. Maybe her mouth. But...

"No," she said in a low voice. Then, louder, as she got off his lap, "No, I don't think so. I think you should go now."

Chapter Eleven

"HOLD MY CALLS," Jamison said to Bobby without so much as a good morning to warm him up. Bobby didn't look surprised, at least not until Jamison added, "and hold all of Ms. Fox's calls, too."

"But...she's --" Bobby began.

Jamison silenced him with a stare. He didn't give a good goddamn what Caite was doing. In about ten minutes she was going to be doing whatever he wanted her to do.

He'd left her apartment when she told him too, his prick so hard it ached. It had stayed that way, on and off, for most of the weekend. He'd edged himself in the shower and at bedtime, then again when he woke up on Sunday, teasing himself almost to completion over and over until he'd had only to lay back and remember Caite's mouth on his in order to come without even touching himself. The climax had been fierce enough to leave him blinded for a few seconds, faint stars swirling in his vision.

It hadn't helped.

He'd woken this morning with another raging hardon and the lingering taste of her teasing him. He'd spent the morning drive thinking of all the ways he was going to deal with what had happened, everything ranging from simply firing her to bending her over his desk and taking her from behind. Now, striding down the hall toward her office, he thought he'd fist his hands in her hair and make her get on her knees. Shit, he thought as he pushed open her door without even knocking, he should give her a severance and be done.

"...Yes, I saw it. Yep. Okay. Sure, no problem," Caite was saying as she turned to stare at him when he burst through her door and shut it behind him. Her eyebrows rose, but she ended the call quickly and before he could say a word, she said, "How rude."

His mouth had opened to let out all the words he'd imagined, but at that simple truth from her, Jamison shut up immediately. He'd never met a woman who could do that to him with little more than an arch of her brow. His fists clenched.

"Sit down," Caite said calmly, pointing to the chair in front of her desk.

He did.

She came around the front to sit on the desk's edge, and oh, fuck him, her plain dark skirt rode up just enough to show off the lacy edge of a pair of thigh high stockings. How had he never noticed her, in all these months? Jamison glowered.

"You look like you have something to say to me, Jamison."

"Oh, I have a lot to say to you."

Caite laughed, damn her. Laughed and shook her head as though he were a naughty school boy brought into the principal's office for pulling a girl's pigtails. Her dark eyes twinkled when she looked back at him.

"You're angry with me?"

He...was. And wasn't. If anything, he was furious with himself for allowing her to do what she'd done. "I'm your boss."

"I thought you said you didn't want me to call you that," she teased.

He drew in a breath, then another to calm himself. "I'm not in the habit of fucking around with my employees."

"I see." Caite crossed her arms and tilted her head to study him.

He waited for her to say something else, but she didn't. "We can't do that again."

"I see." She repeated and shifted a little on the desk, revealing a bit more bare thigh that he did his best to ignore. "Let me ask you something. Why are you so angry about it?"

He took in another breath, but had no words. Being left speechless made him angry. So did the calm way she stared him down. But ultimately, he couldn't articulate an answer.

"I think I know," she said quietly. "It's because you're a man who's always in charge. Right? Always in control. You're used to getting what you want, when you want it, and how. And you don't really trust someone else to get it right."

"If you want to make sure something's done right, you have to do it yourself."

"You like to take care of people."

He had to think about that. His anger had faded in the face of her continued calm. She was like Elise in that way, a foil to his easily ignited fury. "I don't know what you mean."

"You made sure I got home safe. You didn't have to."

"Of course I did. You're mine...You're my employee. It

would've been irresponsible of me to just dump you off in that neighborhood at that time of night." He didn't miss the way his stumbled words had made her smile.

Caite studied him a little longer. "Let me ask you a question, Jamison. Don't you ever get...tired?"

He did. Oh, God, did he ever. Not of things in the office, not being on top of things there. He thrived on that stuff. But in the rest of his life...the never-ending parade of dinner reservations that didn't please women who didn't like to eat, the flowers for others who'd rather have chocolate. The concerts of bands he loved and they'd never heard of and hated.

"Yes," he said. "I do."

Caite resettled herself on the edge of the desk, uncrossing her legs. Her fingers curled into the hem of her skirt, inching it higher while Jamison could only sit there like an idiot, watching. "I dreamed about you. What we did. Kissing you. I dreamed about your kiss, Jamison."

His mouth went dry. His cock, hard. His heart pounded.

Higher, higher, she eased the fabric over her thighs, exposing the sexy-as-hell gartered stockings he'd already glimpsed. He'd never been with a woman who wore stockings like that outside the bedroom and not as part of a costume. He wanted to look away from the promise being revealed between her legs, and had to force himself to meet her eyes.

"You're going to get on your knees for me," Caite whispered. "You're going to put your mouth on me, right here. And make me come with that delicious mouth of yours. Now."

Everything about it screamed wrong. The office setting, her place in the company. The fact that she was the one telling him what to do. And still, Jamison slid from his chair to kneel in front of her, his hands already skimming up the backs of her legs, his mouth already seeking her heat. No thought. No resistance.

Only desire.

She shuddered when he mouthed the softness of her inner thigh just above the stocking. The soft growl of her moan sent another bolt of desire straight through him, tightening his balls and making his dick throb in time to his quickening pulse. When her hand came to rest on top of his head, fingers tangling in his hair, he nipped at her flesh a little harder than he'd intended.

"Fuck, yes," Caite cried, jerking. "Oh. God."

She wore filmy white panties and he hooked a finger in them to pull them aside to get at her pussy. His head spun at the scent of her, but when he got his mouth on her hot flesh, everything else faded away. There was nothing but this. Her heat, the slickness of her pussy on his lips and then fingers when he pushed them inside her. The tight knot of her clit tempted him to suckle gently, and when she cried out again, hips bucking, a little harder.

This was crazy stupid, and not only because they were at work. Because she worked for him, under him...beneath...shit, he was nowhere near on top of things right now. And he had no idea how he'd ended up here or why it was making him so insane.

From down the hall came the sound of ringing phones. The murmur of voices. Shit, he thought, moving away from her. The office door. Not unlocked. And Bobby...

"The door," Jamison said against her.

Caite's fingers tightened in his hair, keeping him close to her. He could pull away if he wanted to. He didn't want to.

"Keep going."

He paused despite the command, picturing Bobby

opening the door and catching his boss going down on the junior assistant. Caite laughed, the full, throaty and rich sound of it making him even harder, if that were possible. Her hand came down to cup his chin, fingers pinching slightly.

"Keep going," Caite said, her gaze bright. Cheeks flushed. Her mouth was wet, like she'd licked it. "I didn't say you could stop."

He'd brought her to orgasm once already by barely doing a thing. He could make her come again, this time with his tongue, in another few minutes. If he wanted to. If he did as she said. If he obeyed.

From behind him, the doorknob rattled. Caite let go of his face. He could've moved away, but did not.

"Make me come, Jamison," Caite whispered, her gaze going over his shoulder as both of them waited for the door to open. It didn't. She looked down at him. "Now."

He feasted on her, a starving man who hadn't known even known he was hungry. She rocked against him. Her clit, tight and hard under his lips and tongue, tempted him to suck it again. He slid a finger inside her. Then another. Stroking upward, slow and easy, not too hard. He wanted to touch himself but did not, masochistically satisfied with the pressure of his cock against the front of his pants making him even crazier.

When her pussy clenched around his fingers, she cried out, low and hoarse. Then again. His name. A framed picture on her desk fell over, and her thighs clamped hard against his head, blocking out the light for a moment. Blocking out sound. All he could see or hear, all he could smell and taste, was Caite's sweet cunt, and in that moment, he'd have happily died with her flavor the last thing he ever tasted.

She leaned back on the desk, her knees falling open to

release him. He sat back on his heels. Caite looked down at him, her eyes glazed and face flushed. She swallowed hard and swept her lips with her tongue. Then she took a deep sighing breath.

"Wow," she said.

She shook herself a little, then sat up straight, pulling down her skirt. She passed a hand over her hair, which had become only a tiny bit disheveled. She smiled at him, saying nothing, and he was glad for it, because that meant he didn't have to answer. He got to his feet, his cock thick with arousal, his balls heavy and aching. He adjusted himself, but it gave little relief. He wanted to be inside her. Or have her mouth on him, her hands, he'd spill himself between her breasts, if she let him, all he could think about, really, was getting off...

Her doorknob rattled again, and this time she looked over his shoulder. "Come in. Hi, Bobby."

"There's a delivery for you. Flowers," Bobby said. "They came from Tommy."

Caite looked surprised. "Ok. Thanks."

When Bobby left the office, she looked at Jamison, still saying nothing. He cleared his throat and unfisted his hands, unaware that he'd been clenching them until she gave them a pointed stare. His fingers ached. He kept himself from holding his hand to his face to breathe her in.

"Was there something else you needed? Boss?"

Damn it, she was teasing him again, though her expression was completely innocent and her tone neutral. Jamison shook his head, backing up a step. If she let her gaze fall to the front of his pants, he thought, he would lock her office door and spin her around, hands on the desk...She kept her eyes on his, that faint smile never twisting or fading.

"No," Jamison said. "Nothing."

Chapter Twelve

CAITE HAD VISITED A MOVIE SET, once, back in college when she'd hung out with all the artsy types who wanted to be directors. Her boyfriend's boyfriend (it had been complicated, yeah) had been hired as an intern on a movie shooting in New York City over the summer, and Caite and Leo had been invited up for the day. It had been hot, the city smelled like urine, and she'd ended up with food poisoning from the craft services table. The movie had gone straight to rental, and she'd never even seen it.

Treasure House was an entirely different matter. Tommy had invited her to come to the site after work on Friday to live tweet during their final filming of the week, a series of teasers that would air to promote the next week's show.

"It's for what we filmed two weeks ago, but will air next week," he explained. "But the network wants us to start getting the word out now. Teasing. You know."

She did. And that was what she was being paid for, to decide what and how and where to put out the message about this show and its three stars. While the three got setup, each filming an individual teaser for several different markets, then group teasers, Caite set up and sent out short video clips and updates to all the social media outlets she could. It wasn't exhausting work, by any means, but even so it <u>was</u> long past five on a Friday night. And even fun work was still work.

"You coming out with us tonight?" Nellie used a makeup remover cloth to swipe at the thick foundation she'd worn for the filming. She eyed Caite. "Tommy says he refuses to go clubbing. Says he wants to have dinner in a nice place with tablecloths, and then...god, go to some art exhibit. I said we could go clubbing after, but he's telling us we got to pick last weekend. Maybe you can change his mind."

Caite looked up from her phone, where she'd been typing in a final update to a fan page. "What makes you think I could do that?"

"He likes you." Nellie simpered. Not a good look for her. "I bet if you said you'd go clubbing, he'd come so he could spend time with you."

Faintly surprised, but only faintly, Caite looked across the room to where Tommy was tucking some things into a messenger bag. He looked good. Faded jeans that hit him in all right places. Black T-shirt that hugged his slim body and revealed strong arms patterned with colorful tattoos. He was not only her type like he'd seen a checklist of what she liked and made himself over to fit it, but he was also surprisingly charming, something she'd never have guessed from watching the show, where he was most often the angry one, yelling at the others to get their shit together.

Shit, she thought, thinking of Jamison. She really did have a type.

Still, what had happened with her boss had been a delicious but definite mistake. He'd barely spoken to her since it had happened and had been keeping his office door closed. There'd been hours of work and little of it completed by the end of the week, even though she'd thrown herself into all of it in order to forget. She got the hint and was sort of glad, too, that he was avoiding her rather than making all of it into something bigger than it had to be. Except...wasn't it? Bigger than it should've been, Caite thought, watching Tommy head toward her with a broad smile on his face. Because she hadn't been able to stop thinking about Jamison's mouth and hands, the look on his face. The sound of his moans.

She was so fucked.

Jamison had blown into her office and then gone down on her like cunnilingus was about to be outlawed and he needed to stock up so he could supply the black market. Yes, she'd basically ordered him to, and yes, she'd made it out as though she were totally in charge, but the truth was, every part of what had happened had shaken her to the core. After he'd made her come with his mouth, her climax so explosive she swore she'd almost lost consciousness for half a minute, he'd gotten to his feet and stared down at her as though waiting for her to say something. Do something. And she's messed it up, hadn't she? Uncertain of what to say, her knees still weak and her mind awhirl with the fact he'd even done it. Again. That he'd given himself up to her. Again. And without getting him off, no reciprocity, nothing for him but a rock-hard dick and probably a set of blue balls. He'd left her office without a word, shutting the door firmly behind him.

But, fucking around with her boss was one thing. Doing it with a client could only lead to worse trouble. Jamison could fire her for what they'd done, but if she screwed this up, it would not only affect her job with Wolfe and Baron, but any job she had in the future. If there was one thing she'd learned fast about working in the media business, it was that fucking celebrities never led to the kind of reputation that did anyone any good.

"Hi," she said, pushing thoughts of her hot-as-hell boss and her future career to the side for a moment. "What's up?"

"Want to come out with us? Dinner at L'Etoile. My treat. Then I'm dragging those yahoos over to the Scott Church gallery show."

"And after that?" She asked, curious. Nellie had gone over to linger with Pax, the two of the doing that annoying whispering thing again.

Tommy looked at his partners. "They want to go clubbing. But shit, I'm tired. Long week, lots of shit went down..."

"Like what?"

He laughed and wagged a finger. "Ah, ah, ah. Can't tell you. You have to tune in."

"Is that where you got the shiner?" Caite touched his cheekbone gently.

Tommy leaned a little closer. "Maybe I got that from my domina."

Caite blinked. Blinked again. She had no idea what to say to that, just that the idea of Tommy having a domina made her tingle in all the right places. Maybe for the wrong reasons, though.

"Relax, cupcake. It's from running into a door in the dark. At least that's what I need to tweet, right?" Tommy grinned. Caite laughed. He took her hand, squeezing lightly. "Come with us. It'll be fun."

"What the hell," Caite said. "Sure. Why not?"

Chapter Thirteen

"WHAT THE HELL WERE YOU THINKING?" Jamison tossed a sheaf of printed pages onto the conference room table. Bobby'd printed out all the latest media updates. They scattered, but he didn't bother to pick them up.

Caite didn't, either. She sat with her hands folded neatly on the table top. Today she wore a crisp white shirt and a black skirt. Black pumps. Her honey blond hair had been pulled into a neat French twist, and in her ears were creamy pearl studs. Her bare throat, uncollared by any jewelry, taunted him.

So did her mouth.

"I'm not sure what you're getting at," she said.

"All of these pictures. The video." Jamison tilted the conference room's laptop toward her to show off the screen, which showed a picture of Caite and that asshole, Tommy whatever-the-fuck-his-name-was, doing shots. And dancing. And laughing. Not kissing, but there was the suggestion of that, too. And lots of commentary about it.

"Treasure House Tommy's new gal pal," he read one of the comments.

Caite snorted. "Oh, brother."

Jamison was as far from laughing as the sun from Pluto. "This isn't what we pay you for."

Caite's laughter cut off abruptly. She sat up higher in her chair, shoulders squaring. One eyebrow lifted, but her fingers didn't even twitch. "What's that supposed to mean?"

"It means that your job's to keep these forons in the public view in a positive light, not...not..." He stopped himself before his voice could rise into a shout, though he wanted it to.

"Not...have fun? Not mix business with pleasure? Not get the buzz going about them? You are aware that last night's Buzzvid clips was re-buzzed more than a thousand times, and that the Wolfe and Baron account got more than five hundred new followers? I don't know how many each of the three Treasure House accounts got, but the comments were in the thousands, too." Her chin went up a little bit. "Compared to the night Nellie got arrested, I'm pretty sure we got a lot more positive growth from a few pictures of us all having a good time."

He didn't want to think about the night Nellie had been arrested. Or what had happened afterwards, in Caite's apartment. Or why what had happened was making him so angry now.

"You're not supposed to be having a good time with...him."

Now both her eyebrows lifted, and her lips parted on a huff of surprise. "I wasn't aware that anything I choose to do when I'm not on the clock is any of your business."

"It is when it reflects on the reputation of this company." Jamison heard the words spitting from his mouth. He even believed them. But at the same time, he knew he was full of shit.

Caite pushed her chair away from the table and stood. Aside from the slight tremble in her voice when she answered him, she was perfectly calm. "If you don't like the way I do my job, Mr. Wolfe, then I suggest you find a replacement."

Silence swelled between them, sharp as glass, as knives. Hot as a dying star. They stared each other down, neither of them moving. Scarcely a blink. Barely a breath.

At last, Caite smoothed the front of her skirt and tucked a non-existent strand of hair behind her ear. "Is that everything? Are you finished?"

"Dammit, Caite, just...listen to me."

She stabbed at the air between them. "No. You listen. I've worked my ass off for this company for eight months, most of those completely under your radar. I've done everything you and Elise asked of me, plus more. You might not like it, but I started taking on a lot more responsibility even before she got sick. So while you might think you've done me some huge favor by letting me take on these clients, the truth is, it's the other way around. You want to talk to me about the reputation of this company? Really? Why. Because you're jealous?"

He *was* jealous. That was the truth of it. He'd been unable to get the taste of her off his tongue for days, and the thought of another man kissing her...touching her...

"Do you think just because we fucked around," Caite said in a low voice, "that you...what? Own me?"

No. That wasn't it at all. Jamison owned an expensive watch, a nice car, furniture. A cellphone. He could never own her. Not that he wanted to, he told himself. And he sure as hell didn't want her to own him.

"What happened between us was unprofessional at best. Stupid at worst," he said. "And has nothing to do with anything else."

Her chin went up. Her eyes flinty. "I agree."

Dammit, that wasn't what he'd wanted her to say. The problem was, Jamison had no idea what he did want her to say. Or do. She'd had him turned upside down from the moment she'd taken control of him, and he hadn't been normal since.

"Like it or not, Ms. Fox, there's a reason why the name of this company is Wolfe and Baron, and it's because I'm the one in charge here. Me. Not you. So you should know your place."

She hesitated, as though she meant to say something else, then let out a low, soft sound. Her expression softened, a shift in her gaze. A tiny quirk of her mouth that wasn't a smile, but at least was better than a frown or the cold, grim line of her anger.

"Nothing happened with us," Caite murmured so softly he almost didn't hear it.

In a way he wished he hadn't, because hearing it meant that somehow, she knew it mattered to him. "Just keep your personal life personal, Ms. Fox. Not on company time."

For another few seconds, he thought she meant to say more, but whatever words had filtered to her tongue she bit back. He hated the cold flatness in her look, as though they barely knew each other. Well. That was the truth, wasn't it? They barely did.

So why then, he thought as he watched her leave the room without so much as a glance behind her, did he feel like Caite Fox knew him better than anyone ever had?

Chapter Fourteen

INDEPENDENT.

Mouthy.

You're an aggressive, intimidating bitch.

The words of not just one but a few of her boyfriends echoed in her memory as Caite at last gave up the pretense of trying to work and shut down her computer. Her phone had been blessedly silent for the past few hours, the updates she'd scheduled getting a sufficient number of shares and comments, but nothing she had to handle. She could give in, call it a day. Go home.

Nothing waited for her there but a bottle of wine she'd have to drink by herself -- never a great idea. And darkness. And quiet. Even the idea of a bubble bath with candles and a good book didn't really appeal to her. She didn't want to go home. Not alone, anyway.

For the first time in years, really, Caite was tired of being alone. Her longest relationship had lasted four years and ended amicably enough a couple years ago when she and Dallas had both agreed that his promotion and consequent transfer to California was as good at time as any for them to either make a permanent commitment or to call it quits. Ending it as friends had seemed the better deal. Since then, she'd dated. Not consistently, but a lot. A few, not many, had become "boyfriends." But most of them had been nothing except a way to pass the time until she'd grown tired of the parade of first dates that had never been good enough to turn into second ones. Getting off the dating carousel had been a relief, and being alone had been a choice.

Now, though, all she could think about was...well, not the sex. Though it had been amazing. Fantastic. Mind-blowing. But not the sex. The connection.

She and Jamison had not fucked like strangers getting naked together for the first time. Hell. They hadn't even fucked, technically. He'd give her pleasure -- twice! And left without it being reciprocated. And yet those two times with him had been more erotic, more fulfilling and more mean-ingful than a double fistful of simultaneous orgasms and the afterglow of pillow talk. They had started from different places and ended the same way, yet during it had met in the middle and found each other as though they'd clasped hands in a dark room and shown each other the way to the light.

"Oh, ugh. Gross," Caite murmured. "Stupid. Fairy tales and firesides, this is not."

But...what harm could it do to fantasize about it? All the months she'd worked here, her boss had certainly tantalized her daydreams. The reality of him had been even better. So what if it wasn't going to happen again, it wasn't meant to last, it had been shifting, scattering castles of dust. So what if he'd made it beyond clear that kneeling in front of her had been...wrong. Unprofessional, he'd said. And stupid.

Stupid, all right. Stupid to think a man like Jamison

Wolfe would ever be able to give her what she wanted and needed. Still. That didn't mean she couldn't remember that just for those brief moments, it had happened.

He had kneeled for her.

And he'd loved it.

With a groan, Caite settled back in her chair and closed her eyes to try and chase away the memory of his mouth on her. His glazed look when he'd stared up at her from between her legs. When he'd turned and left without so much as a hand job, all at her command. She couldn't stop herself from touching the pulse beating in the base of her throat. Then her wrists, where she pressed against the throbbing flow of her blood that had gone heated and swift in her veins at the thought of his kiss.

It could never work. Boss, employee, they were worlds apart even without that impropriety. But Jamison had given her a taste of what Caite had always craved and had been unable to articulate or even admit to herself until he had responded to her commands. And now, having tasted it, the idea of never having it again was enough to make her want to throw something on the floor and break it.

She'd finished her work hours ago but had not gone home, and why? Hoping to catch a glimpse of Jamison, who'd been so clearly avoiding her. That more than anything had convinced her of his disgust. Jamison Wolfe was not a man to avoid anyone, ever, yet he'd almost made a career of pretending she didn't exist.

Now the office was quiet. Bobby gone. Jamison might have left too, but she didn't think so. With a shivering sigh, the residual memory of his mouth on her cunt making her breath catch, Caite put both her hands flat on the desk. Thinking about every cruel thing any man had ever said to her.

You should know your place.

That last had hurt worse than anything else. Her place? What was her place, exactly. Below, beneath, less than? And why? Because she was a woman?

"Fuck that," she said aloud, though the harsh words didn't chase away the taste of bitterness.

It had been two weeks since Jamison had blown up at her about going out with Tommy. She needed to talk to him. If nothing else, they needed to get some things straight so they could keep working together. Caite had never been the sort of woman to let things like this slide. It had earned her a lot of heat from past lovers who hadn't appreciate her honesty or forthrightness, but...Jamison was unlike any of them had ever been.

He was different.

The thought of that alone was enough to get her moving. Her bare thighs rubbed together above the tops of her stockings, and the click-click of her high heels on the hallway's tile floor tickled her eardrums. He'd be able to hear her coming.

She knocked on his door and waited for him to reply before opening it. She didn't bother with peeking around the doorframe. She walked right in and closed the door firmly behind her, making sure to lock it.

"We need to talk," she said.

He looked as wary as she felt, but nodded and gestured to the chair in front of his desk. Caite took a seat, sitting on the edge. Back straight. Hands folded on her lap. Not sure what she meant to say until the words came out.

"I've had seven lovers in my life," she began without preamble. "A few one night stands. Two of them were what I might consider serious, long-term. None of them ever, ever did for me what you've done. I'd never asked it of any of them, not outright, though in retrospect I guess there was always that element there. None of them ever responded to me the way you did, Jamison. None of them ever made me feel the way you did. I thought you should know."

He said nothing for a few seconds, so long she began to wonder if he meant to say nothing at all. Then he cleared his throat. "I was married at twenty-four. It lasted two years. I haven't had a girlfriend since that lasted longer than a year. Most less than that. The women I've dated, including my ex, all seemed really happy to let someone else do all the work. All the heavy lifting, I guess you could say. And I thought I liked that, for a long time. Having things my way. Getting what I wanted."

"Most people like getting their own way."

He laughed a little shamefacedly, and shook his head. "You can't run a relationship like you run a business deal."

"No," Caite said. "I guess you can't."

There was more silence, less awkward than before. Jamison sat back in his chair. Caite kept her position upright, stiff. Professional. She wasn't ready to relax, not just yet.

"What I said to you was wrong," he said.

Her eyebrows rose.

"About knowing your place." His voice dropped. Regretful. "It was arrogant of me, and it wasn't what I meant. I just...you...damn."

"I what?" She leaned forward a little bit, her posture softening despite her desire to keep up a cold front.

Jamison looked at her. "You came at me so hard, Caite. You're this little bitty thing, and you have this huge presence."

"You're not used to a girl like me," she said, tilting her head to study him. Her heart thumped a little faster. She couldn't stop herself from grinning, just a little.

"No. I'm definitely not." He paused, his expression hardening. "And I'm sure not used to being...to letting..."

He trailed off, and she didn't push him. They shared more silence. Staring at each other.

"If it helps," she said finally, "I'm not used to a guy like you, either."

"I don't think workplace relationships are appropriate, especially between a boss and employee."

She nodded, not surprised, but feeling a pinch in her guts just the same. "I understand."

"What if it doesn't work out?" Jamison continued, stony faced. "Working together could put a whole lot of pressure on things."

Her eyebrows rose again, but only for a second or so. "My last boyfriend broke up with me because I wouldn't do his laundry. He said, what use was staying together when he knew he'd never marry me if I couldn't just do it for him."

"Are you asking me if I'll expect you to do my laundry?"

"I'm pointing out that relationships end for all sorts of dumb reasons. Working together isn't necessarily going to make it harder. Or easier." Caite shrugged. "It just means, maybe, that we'll have to be extra honest with each other, that's all. About what we want and expect. And that's not such a bad thing, is it? To start off being honest?"

"I do get tired," Jamison said after a few more beats of silence she timed by the beating of her heart. "What you asked me before...yes. I get tired."

Her guts tumbled and twisted inside her, but Caite kept herself calm by breathing in through her nose, out through her mouth. In, out, three, four. "You would like to give up, once in a while. Let someone else take control."

He shuddered, and she thought for sure he was going

to deny it. Worse, that his lip would curl, that he'd send her from the room. Instead, after a long, long moment, he nodded.

An emotion so fierce she didn't know how to name it leaped inside her; in the next second at the sight of Jamison's slow, sexy smile, Caite knew what it was. Joy. He licked his lips, never looking away from her.

"And I do my own laundry."

"<u>Would</u> you do *mine*?" she asked, meaning to sound light, but her voice dipped low and husky and raw.

Another hesitation, but something gleamed in his eyes. "Yes. If you wanted me to."

"To my specifications? Exactly?" She kept her hands clasped tight, fingers intertwined.

"Yes."

"And what if you didn't do it the way I wanted it done?"

"I guess," Jamison said after a hesitation, "I'd have to make it up to you."

Her cunt clenched at the thought of it. She swept her lower lip with her tongue and reveled in watching his eyes track the motion. "This is complicated."

"I know."

"And you don't like it," she added. "I understand why."

He nodded.

She got up from her chair and went around the desk, helpless against the impulse to touch him. To put her hands on him. To make him real to her in a way he hadn't been for the past eight months when he'd been nothing more than a shouting voice and a signature on her paycheck.

"Do you want me to stop?" She cupped his face and tipped it to hers.

"No."

She brushed a kiss against his mouth. "Do you want to make me happy?"

Something shifted and shone in his gaze again; something facile and slippery and uncertain that she could see him visibly struggle to subdue. "Yes. I don't know why. But I do."

Caite's laugh snagged in her throat on something suspiciously like a sob. She kissed him, this time harder. Longer. Her tongue quested inside his mouth, and when he at last sucked hers, she moaned against him. Then she pulled away, breathing hard but standing straight. Shoulders squared. She looked him in the eyes.

"Take me to your place. And show me how much you want to make me happy."

Chapter Fifteen

JAMISON TOOK her to his place, because she'd told him to. If the size of his apartment impressed her, Caite didn't show it. She shrugged out of her coat inside the front door and tossed it onto a chair, then turned to him.

"Bedroom."

"Upstairs," he said. "The loft."

She laughed. "I never guessed you for a man with a...loft."

"What's wrong with a loft?" Jamison asked, not sure why he was laughing, too, only that no woman had ever both aroused and amused him, lifted him and made him lighter, as Caite.

"Nothing's wrong with a loft. It's just so artistic."

But she changed her mind a few minutes later when he showed her his loft, which was not an open space looking over the main living area, but an enclosed bedroom and bathroom reached by a curving staircase. The loft part of it was a cozy balcony furnished with a couple of chairs and a good reading lamp, along with a heavy cherry bookcase stuffed with all his favorite titles.

"I love it," Caite said, looking at the shelves of books, then at him. "It's everything I thought of you. A loft that's not typical, but practical. And lovely. And well-loved."

He snorted soft laughter at that last bit. "You know all of me so well."

"Not all of you. Not yet," Caite said with a glance at him over her shoulder as she went into his bedroom. She looked over the bed. "You have a housekeeper?"

"No."

She smoothed the bed. "You make your bed this neatly yourself?"

"Yes," Jamison said and found another laugh.

It could've made all of this seem silly, that laugh, but when she joined him, all it did was make all of this somehow better. He crossed to her and took her in his arms. He kissed her, wondering if she would pull away or chastise him. If she'd put him in the place of...well, a slave, he guessed, thinking of some of the porn he'd seen but had never really liked.

Nothing Caite had done so far had made him feel less than a man, though, and she melted into his touch now with a small, shivering sigh that made his cock twitch. He'd been half hard all day long, his balls heavy and aching with arousal. When she slipped her hands up his chest to link behind his neck, Jamison did what felt natural -- he lifted her up to carry her to the bed where he lay her down care-fully. He moved over her, their kisses getting harder until she nipped at his lower lip.

"Slower," Caite commanded in that low, silky voice that was like a fingertip trailing all the way down his spine to his balls.

Jamison moved his mouth from hers to nuzzle and nibble at her neck. The ridge of her collarbone, exposed by her neckline. The first hint of her breasts. Then he stopped. Didn't move. One knee pressed between her legs, nudging upward, then still.

Caite let out a low, frustrated laugh. "Not that slow."

Then they were laughing again, and it had been so long since he'd laughed in bed with a woman...hell, had he ever? He nuzzled her again, sliding a hand up to cup her breast. They stayed that way for a few minutes.

She put her lips to his ear. "Get on your back."

He rolled, taking her with him so she straddled him. She opened his belt and button on the pants, then the zipper, working efficiently but stopping to look into his eyes as her hand slipped inside. His straining cock peeked out from the top of his briefs, already slick at the head. He thought if she touched him, he'd embarrass himself like a virgin in the backseat of his dad's Mustang on prom night. When she curved her hand around him through the fabric of his briefs, he did indeed buck upward with a groan.

Caite moved back, off him. "Take off your clothes."

He couldn't move right away, paralyzed at the loss of her touch until he forced himself to sit up and shrug out of his shirt. Then, standing, he took off his socks. Pants. In his briefs he paused, thumbs in the waistband, and instead of shucking them off and diving on top of her, he remembered what she'd said. _Slower_.

He went slower.

Caite's smile made it worth it. She sat up on the bed, crooking a finger. "Come here."

He did, crawling up the bed toward her, but she held him back by putting her foot on his chest. Her toes curled, lightly. He waited, impatient but forcing himself to do it anyway. She sat up and ran a fingertip down his shoulder, across his chest. Tweaked his nipple gently. Then harder.

"Do you like pain, Jamison?"

His laugh was harsher this time. "I don't know."

"Do you want to find out?"

His balls tightened at the thought of it. His cock twitched. "Do you?"

"I've never hit anyone on purpose," Caite whispered, voice shaking just enough to make him want to kiss her again and again, to never stop. "I'm not sure how I feel about it, to be honest."

This surprised him enough to sit back. Jamison swallowed. He didn't want to dwell on what the hell he was doing here with her, what she'd awakened in him. Couldn't think too hard about it, or how he'd be an idiot about things, he knew it. But he had to ask her.

"You said nobody'd ever responded to you the way I do."

"No. I mean, yes." She laughed. "Nobody ever has. It's intoxicating."

"But you've done...this...before?"

He was grateful he hadn't had to explain himself in greater detail. She got it right away. Caite shook her head slowly. Solemnly.

"If you mean...take control?" she asked delicately, and he couldn't be sure if he were grateful for her hesitation in giving this a more descriptive name or if he wanted to hear her say it out loud.

"Dominate," Jamison coughed on the word, his cock losing some of its thickness with the words.

"Some things," Caite said quietly, "don't need to be named to enjoy them."

They stared at each other. She smiled, urging his own. Whatever it was, she made him want to do it. To please her. To give to her. To give in.

"I've never," he began, and she put a fingertip to his lips.

"Shh. I know. On your back," Caite said. "Hands above your head."

In the past he'd indulged lovers who'd wanted to ride him, but this was different. This was...everything. When she shimmied out of her panties and straddled him, her skirt pushed to her hips, the stockings sleek against him, his fingers gripped the wooden spindles of his headboard hard enough to make it creak.

"Condom?" she asked matter of factly.

"Bedside table...how did you know I'd..."

"I was hoping. You'd have been a very sad man if you didn't have anything," she whispered, reaching, the motion putting her delectable breasts within reach of his mouth. She laughed when he made to kiss her there, and pulled away with a condom in her hand. "Ah, ah, ah."

In seconds she'd sheathed him. A moment after that, she'd settled herself on him with a groan he echoed. His prick throbbed inside her and again, Jamison feared he might spill. She gripped him with internal muscles, rocking, and again he made the headboard complain.

"Slow," she whispered and reached to unpin her hair. It tumbled around her shoulders in waves of deep, honey blond, and although he longed to sink his fingers into it, Jamison kept his grip tight on the headboard, just as she'd told him to.

She fucked him slowly, every rock and shift of her bringing him to the edge, only to have the pleasure settle back again. Caite closed her eyes, head tipping back. She hadn't unbuttoned more than a couple buttons on her blouse, just enough to give him a hint of cleavage. She ran her hands over her breasts, then her belly, sliding her fingers between them to stroke her clit as her hips moved faster.

She opened her eyes. "I came so hard when your mouth was on me, do you know that?"

"I'm glad," he found the strength to say.

Caite moved faster, biting her lower lip in concentration. Her eyes met his, not looking away. He let himself drown in their darkness.

"I want you to feel good, Jamison. The way you made me feel."

"I...do..."

"Tell me how good."

He fucked upward, unable to help it. "Feels so damned good, Caite. I want to come."

"I want you to come," she said. "But not just yet. Let me..."

"Oh, yeah."

She cried out, low and raspy. Her pussy bore down on him, milking him, and he fought to keep himself from finishing even though the world was tipping from the effort. He wanted to come, but his desire to feel her come around his cock was greater than his need to climax. He watched her ride him, her head tipped back, eyes closed in abandon. She was the most beautiful thing he'd ever seen in that moment, when at last she shook with pleasure and cried out his name. The sound of it triggered him at last, and he finished with hoarse shout.

She covered him with her body for a few seconds, her hair sweeping over him, before she rolled to the side with a contented sigh. "Damn."

Jamison let go of the headboard finally, and rolled onto his side to face her. Tucking her hand under her cheek, Caite smiled at him. With her other hand, she pushed away some hair from his forehead and let her fingertip run down his nose to tap lightly on his lips before she got up and swung her legs over the edge of the bed.

She was...leaving?"

"Wait a minute," Jamison said.

She glanced at him over her shoulder, already pinning up her hair again. "Hmmm?"

"You can stay."

Caite laughed. "I know I can. But I'm not going to."

He sat up, confused and hating it. "Why not?"

"Because," she said as she leaned to kiss him softly, "you will be a grouch in the morning and we'll have to have some sort of weird discussion about what this is, or what we are, and you'll be awkward about us working together. And I just can't deal with it, Jamison. I've just had the best sex of my life, ever, and I'd love to bask in the afterglow, but I know you. You're going to..."

She paused with a low hitch in her breath, the confident woman he'd come to crave fading for a moment before she visibly shook herself into self assurance again. She looked him in the eyes, cupping his face before letting him go. Stepping out of reach.

"I don't want regret," Caite said. "I couldn't stand it, to be honest. It would kill me."

"I don't regret it." The moment he said it, he knew it was true. "Don't go. Stay here with me."

She eyed him, and he could see that as reluctant as she was to agree, she wanted to. "Jamison..."

He didn't try to reach for her, but he got off the bed and moved close enough that she could touch him, if she wanted to. "I'm not a man who takes no for an answer."

Caite lifted an eyebrow, but didn't disagree.

"I know what I want, and how to get it. It's kind of a thing of mine--"

"I've noticed," she said drily. "You kind of have a reputation."

He smiled. "I want you to stay with me tonight. And in the morning, I'll make you breakfast. Anything you like."

"French toast? With powdered sugar?"

"If that's what you want."

Caite crossed her arms, looking stern. "Do you *have* powdered sugar?"

"No. Or eggs. Or milk. Or bread. But I'll get up early enough in the morning to get to the store before you wake up, so I can buy everything I need to make you what you want."

"...Is that what a submissive man does?" Caite asked, almost as though she were musing.

"I don't know," Jamison said and finally took her in his arms to tug her closer for a long, lingering kiss. "But I know it's what I do."

Chapter Sixteen

WHEN JAMISON WOLFE committed to something, he did it at full speed. It shouldn't have surprised Caite, not after watching him work. But discovering that he was very much the same way at play was still a delight and a wonder, and something she was going to need more than a few weeks to get used to, no matter how exciting those weeks had been. She'd had devoted boyfriends who'd bowed to her every whim and aggressive lovers that had fought her on everything. She'd never been with a man who could spend the afternoon completely catering to her every need without ever asking her what she wanted as flawlessly and confidently as if he'd downloaded her personal instruction manual, and then spend the night on his knees in front of her while she ordered him to edge himself to orgasm over and over until only the barest breath of her on his cock sent him over the edge.

The combination was heady and electric, and she couldn't get enough, but...

"Enough," Caite breathed as his fingers slowed inside her. Her orgasm had flooded her entire body that time.

Boneless and sated, she sank into the couch cushions and tried to catch her breath.

Jamison kissed her mouth, then got up to pour them both glasses of orange juice from the carafe on the tray he'd set on the coffee table. He'd made her breakfast, hand-fed her bits of French toast and sausage, then made love to her until they both fell asleep on the thick rug in front of the fireplace. Then he'd woken her with his hands and mouth and brought her to another rousing orgasm, and now he was hydrating her.

She could love this man, Caite thought blearily. The idea of it was enough to make her sit up straight. She took the juice. "Thanks, baby."

Jamison brushed her sweat-damp hair off her forehead and kissed her again. "Have to keep my princess happy."

Caite eyed him. "Princess, huh?"

His answer was a cheeky grin. He'd never called her mistress. She hadn't asked him to. She'd thought about asking him to call her Domina, but hadn't done that either. Yet.

"Sure. You don't like it?"

"It's better than pooky sweetums or something like that," she agreed.

Naked, Jamison got up to adjust the gas fireplace flames. The view was stunning. Long, lean legs, smooth skin, firm ass. The dimples at the base of his spine sent her heart into palpitations.

"You should always be naked in my presence," Caite said.

"That would make it awkward for our clients," Jamison began as he turned to look at her, and just like that, whatever this had become flared again between them.

Thick and heavy with promise, electric. Volcanic. In three heartbeats he was at her feet, kneeling with that perfect ass resting on his heels, his blue eyes gone dark with desire. His pulse throbbing, matched by hers. He leaned to her as she reached for him, and when he put his cheek against her thigh, her fingers buried deep in the thickness of his hair, Caite had never felt so complete.

He stayed like that for a few seconds only. Then his shoulders heaved with a giant breath. He looked at her, mouth thin.

"What, baby," she asked. "What is it?"

"This..." He ran his hands up her legs to tuck his fingers beneath her thighs. He shook his head.

There was no question it turned her on to have him on his knees for her, but it unnerved her to see him struggle with it. They'd played a bit over the past three weeks with commands and scenes, things they'd seen in porn. But the pomp and ceremony of what Caite refused to call by a four-letter acronym didn't appeal to either one of them. It had become something both simpler and vastly more complicated than that -- Caite asked. Jamison complied.

"I like to make you happy," Jamison said. "I don't know why. I just do."

"You do make me happy."

He shook his head a little, cutting his gaze. "It's more than that, Caite. In the past few weeks, I've felt...free."

Her heart lodged in her throat. She sat up take his face in her hands and turn it toward hers. She kissed him softly. Then again, a little harder. "Me too."

But he still looked troubled, and she didn't know what to say or do to make that change. They sat that way for a moment longer. Then she traced his eyebrows with her fingertip. The curve of his mouth, which finally turned to a smile.

"Why put a name on this?" She murmured. "What other people do is their own business. What we do is ours.

So long as we're both making each other happy, do we have to think too hard about it?"

"I haven't had much experience making people happy," Jamison answered, sort of sourly.

His frown charmed her so much she had to kiss him again. "You're good at it. Trust me."

They were quiet together for a while after that, the sort of easy silence that falls between lovers who don't need words to say how they feel. Her hand smoothed over his hair. His breath blew warm on her skin as he rested his head in her lap. They had to get up, she thought lazily. They had to move, to shower, get dressed. But for now it was enough to stay right where they were.

Chapter Seventeen

THE DAILY LISTS were long and detailed and precise, written in Caite's looping hand with the fountain pen she'd snagged from his desk and taken as her own. Random things. Ridiculous things, sort of, which made them all the more important to him for some reason.

Think of her at a certain time on the clock. Wear a specific tie. Order something particular for lunch delivery. Spend an hour exercising, then treat himself to his favorite beer. Text her a picture of his socks. She was big on pictures of what he was wearing, which was really silly since she could see his clothes at any time. It wasn't the photos themselves, Caite had told him, whispering in the darkness with her hand idly stroking his cock and stopping just before he came, so that he'd been floating in a haze of arousal he thought might kill him -- and that he'd gladly die. It wasn't the photos but the fact he was doing it for her because she'd asked it of him. No matter what it was. She liked making the lists because she said it meant he'd be thinking about how to please her all day long. Like foreplay for hours.

As if he wouldn't be thinking about her all day anyway, Jamison thought. Caite had captivated him. Intoxicated him. He was...addicted.

He thought he might even be in love.

They hadn't talked about that. Not about love, or even what this was between them. With Elise out of the office and Bobby settled in his desk down the hall, it would've been so easy for Jamison and Caite to sneak their private life into the workplace. He'd thought about it, of course. That first day in her office when she'd ordered him to go down on her haunted him, sending him a few times to the men's room to force his dick into submission with a cold-water face dunk. Their days at work, however, by unspoken mutual agreement, might simmer with sexual tension because of the lists and the simple fact that with every look they set each other on fire, but they kept themselves as professional as possible.

At least, as much as he hated to admit it, with the Treasure House clients bringing Wolfe and Baron more attention and new clients every day, it was easier to keep themselves busy and focused on the job and not each other than it might've been even a few months ago. And it wasn't like they didn't have any time together away from the job. Three or four nights a week, she came to his place, and their nights were taken up with getting to know each other in every way it was possible for two people to do it. He'd have been glad for more, but Caite had been firm about keeping things professional in the office. She said they needed their time and space away from each other, especially since they worked together. And she was right. She was right about most things he needed or wanted, even if he didn't know it himself.

Or wouldn't admit it. She was good at that, too. Finding all his secrets, even ones he himself hadn't known he had. In only a few short weeks, Caite Fox had turned him inside out.

Jamison scanned the new list she'd left for him that morning before she left to do a few site visits. Today's was shorter than usual. One task only.

Surprise me with something that shows you know me.

For a moment, stumped, Jamison stared at the words on the paper. Caite had proven herself to know him, time and time again, in ways he'd never failed to find amazing. It didn't shock him that she might want him to know her a little, too. The question was going to be, could he do it?

Chapter Eighteen

"So you see," Caite said as she demonstrated, "You have to keep your finger pressed to the screen to record. You only get a few seconds. And then the video records, and it makes a loop."

Margeurite Miles was one of the leading concert pianists in the country. She'd forged her name as a child prodigy, performing complicated pieces of music even masters found difficult, and had continued her career by creating an image of herself as something beyond the stereotypical classical musician. Her shows were full of theatrics and special celebrity guests, air cannons of confetti or bubble machines.

She was also technologically incompetent.

"Like this?" Mags held up her phone, a brand new model she'd brought into Caite's office without even taking it out of the box.

"No...you have to hold in the...press on the..." Caite demonstrated.

Mags tried again. And failed. But she didn't get frustrated, which was a quality Caite appreciated about her.

The older woman wanted to reach out to her younger audience, and if that meant Connex and Buzzvid and Twitter, by golly, she was going to learn how to do it.

Caite had already gone over how to schedule social media updates and some basic training, but so far, Mags was simply not getting it. With a sigh, Caite shook her head. Mags laughed, embarrassed.

"I'll practice." Mags held up both hands, wiggling her fingers. "I'm supposed to be good with my hands."

Caite laughed and patted her on the shoulder. "You'll get the hang of it, I'm sure."

"Is our time up?" Mags peered at her phone. "Darn, is the time even right on this thing?"

"The time should almost always be right on that because it's supposed to update automatically. Even if you change time zones." Caite slid a checklist of phone apps and websites across the desk. Normally she'd have emailed it, but Mags never checked her email.

Still, she'd become one of Caite's favorite clients. Helping Mags reach and entertain a new audience felt good. As she showed the older woman out, Mags shuffled in her purse, pulling out an envelope.

"This is for you. Two tickets to one of my shows." Mags looked at her. "You have a date, right?"

"I think I can find one."

"If not, I have a really handsome nephew about your age," Mags began as they walked down the hall, only to be interrupted by Jamison coming out of his office. "Oh, Mr. Wolfe. Hello!"

"What's this about tickets to your show?"

Caite held up the envelope. "Mags gave us two tickets. She's trying to set me up with her nephew. Think I can get a better offer than that?"

"My nephew is very handsome," Mags said again,

"though...now that I think about it, he's not very funny. Takes after my sister that way, which is really too bad. A man who makes you laugh is a keeper."

"I think we can find you someone who can make you laugh," Jamison said with a straight face, his gaze piercing Caite's.

Mags waved a hand as she headed for the lobby, leaving them both behind. "Just so long as he doesn't make you cry!"

Caite watched her go, waiting until Mags had turned the corner before facing him. "You do make me laugh."

"Good." He pulled her close for a kiss, nuzzling her neck until she gasped and pushed him away.

"You're the one who said we had to be discreet in the office," Caite muttered, shaking a finger. "Though I'm sure Bobby's got his suspicions."

"Nobody's here to see us. Mags was your last client of the day. And I told Bobby that once she was gone, he could knock off early, too." Jamison bent to nuzzle her again.

Caite held him off and took a step back, out of reach. Since Jamison had been so adamant in the beginning about workplace relationships, she'd made sure to keep any sort of physical hanky panky to a minimum. Partly to assuage him. Partly to frustrate him. It had been delicious.

"So you think that you're going to get lucky in the office? Is that it? A little afternoon delight?"

"A guy can dream, can't he?" He flashed her a charming grin that threatened to melt her panties, though she didn't so much as bat an eyelash to show him how hot she thought it was.

"Did you finish the list I gave you this morning?"

And just like that, the inferno that constantly simmered between them flared to life.

"I did. Come with me."

His grin, wide and bright, made Caite melt, mostly because she'd seen him smile at a lot of people, and he didn't look at anyone the way he looked at her. No man had ever looked at her the way Jamison did. It didn't only set her on fire. It made her feel adored. Cherished.

Loved.

Which scared her, but she wasn't going to think about that now. Instead she followed him into the conference room, where she let out a small gasp at what lay in front of her. She turned to him, stunned.

"You...did this? All of this?"

His smile was her answer. Caite took an unsteady step toward him, not sure if she meant to laugh or cry. Surprise me, she'd told him. He'd done more than that. He'd blown her mind.

Jamison had set the table with a vase of crimson roses in a crystal vase tied with a thick purple ribbon. The flowers were standard, any woman might love red roses, but the ribbon...that was all Caite. Two plates of thin china, matching the ones she had in her apartment, held thick slices of cherry cheesecake. Her favorite. Two wine glasses, filled with red wine. A platter of savory crackers and sliced cheeses, along with small bowls of Greek olives.

"Cheesecake for dinner?"

"Dessert first, because you're the sort of woman who breaks the rules," he said. "And just a little appetizer. Dinner reservations are for later, at Serrano. And tickets to see that guy you like. The one who plays the guitar."

Caite couldn't move. She tried to breathe, and found the best she could manage was tiny sips of air. She was going to burst into tears, and she didn't want to do that. She swallowed her emotions around the lump in her throat, and opened her mouth to thank him.

"There's more," he said before she could say a word. "Open the box."

She'd missed the sleek black box, about the size of a cereal box though made of much heavier cardboard. Another purple ribbon was tied around it in a crisp bow. Caite went around the table to look at it.

Jamison followed her. "Open it."

All at once, she didn't want to. Her hands shook so much she had to fist them, hiding them in the folds her full skirt. She couldn't look at him. He'd done so much, all of it proving her knew her exactly. Whatever was in this box would be more of the same, or a disappointment, and Caite was suddenly terrified of being disappointed.

"Jamison," she said, but couldn't make herself continue.

He fit himself along her body from behind, his hands slipping around her to press flat on her belly and pull her against him. His kiss found the smooth curve of her neck and shoulder. He didn't nuzzle or try to feel her up. He held her. Offering her his warmth. His support, though he couldn't possibly know her reason for hesitating. Could he?

"I'm scared to open it," she whispered.

"Don't be scared."

"What if I don't like it, whatever it is?"

His gaze, dark with desire, softened. "You wanted me to surprise you. To show I know you. I'm doing the best I can."

"And so far, everything...is perfect." She twisted in his arms to kiss him.

"Shouldn't I be the one who's worried if you won't like it?" His tone was light, but she saw a hint of seriousness in his eyes. "What if I failed?"

"What if you didn't?" Caite asked. "What if you got it just right, because you know me so well?"

Something was changing between them, right there in that moment. Caite could feel it. So could Jamison, she saw it in his eyes and heard it in the catch of his breath. She felt it in his mouth on hers, firm yet somehow searching.

"Open the box, Caite. Please."

So, she did.

Chapter Nineteen

JAMISON DIDN'T IMAGINE her sigh of relief when she undid the ribbon and lifted the box's lid to reveal a matching bra, panty and garterbelt set of black lace and emerald green satin. Caite lifted the scanty underthings from their nest of crumpled tissue paper, along with the pair of sheer nude stockings. The salesgirl had assured him the nude was better than black -- Caite was almost certain to already have several sets of black stockings, but might need a neutral pair. It had been a bunch of technical jargon to Jamison, but the girl in the shop had convinced him.

"You know my size," Caite said.

"That was the easy part." Jamison watched her stroke the material. She was smiling. That was a good sign. "But there's more."

She looked up at him, then set aside the lingerie carefully on the table. She pulled aside the tissue paper. His stomach lurched, waiting for her discover what else he'd bought. Two items, chosen even more carefully than the stockings.

Caite pulled out the first and gave a delighted laugh as she held up the red satin and let it run through her fingers. At first she held it to her throat, but before he had to explain what the scarf's true purpose was, she figured it out. Snapping it taught between her fists, she held it up.

"A blindfold." She sounded pleased and yes, surprised. Something like tears glinted in her eyes for a second before she blinked them away. "How naughty."

"There's one more thing."

Brushing the satin against her lips for a second before putting it aside, Caite nodded. This time, when she found the final item, she gasped. Mouth open, she stared at him for a few seconds before getting herself under control. She pulled her hand out of the box and held up what she'd brought out with her.

Jamison had never been in a sex toy shop before this morning, when he went in to fulfill Caite's list. The rows of dildos and vibrators hadn't turned his head. Nor had the selection of fetish-wear, most of it cheaply made. She was worth more than a catsuit that would split at the seams the first time she wore it. He'd about given up, but then in the back room, a separate section of the store run by a different vendor that was renting space, he'd found what he was looking for. Hand-crafted of smooth, supple leather. No buckles, but instead thin silk cord wound through punched holes. The cuffs were unique and beautiful, just like Caite.

But they weren't for her.

"Jamison," she said in low voice, letting her fingers toy with the cords that closed the cuffs. "Oh, my god. Oh."

Sewn into the leather's edge were genuine pearls, three on each cuff. He could've special-ordered them with other jewels, diamonds, rubies. Embroidered with his name, or hers. But the moment Jamison had seen the pearl-edged cuffs, he'd known they were the ones.

Caite brought them to her face and sniffed, eyes closed. "I love the smell of leather. I love pearls."

"I know."

"These are gorgeous," she murmured, holding the cuffs to her cheek for a second or so before looking at him. "And unexpected. I mean, completely not at all what I was expecting. You really surprised me."

When Jamison was closing in on the end of a deal, his world shifted. Vision narrowed. When he had the other guy in his sights, everything going the way he wanted it to, the guarantee of success became close he could taste it, thick like honey but sweeter. In those moments, winning, he felt like he was in a different universe. He felt that way now, too, though instead of sweetness an anxious bitterness teased his tongue.

"You'd like to use them on me," he said aloud. He didn't stutter or stumble; the words came out of him with as much confidence as anything he'd ever said while sealing a negotiation. On the inside though, everything had gone dark and swimming. Uncertain. "You'd like to bind my hands, Caite. You'd like to get me on my knees with my hands behind my back, using those cuffs."

A slow creeping flush eased up her throat to paint her face. She licked her lips, and the sight of her tongue move across them sent a wave of desire flooding straight to his already half-hard cock. She stroked the leather again, then the shimmering, creamy pearls.

"And they don't lock," she said under breath, almost as though she were talking to herself. "You'd be bound more by my desire than by the cuffs themselves. Oh, fuck, Jamison. Oh, God, I love them. But will you?"

Of everything they'd done, her desire to control him in this way had been the one thing he'd felt certain he'd deny her, if she asked. The lists, the commands, the hours he'd spent worshipping her body before ever even getting close to achieving his own release -- all of that had seemed like something from a dream. If you'd asked him months ago if he'd ever submit sexually to a woman in that way, Jamison might've laughed or even thrown a punch, depending on who was doing the asking. Nothing Caite had asked of him had ever felt cheap or abusive or castrating. But this...

"It's crossing the line," he said.

Caite nodded, then tilted her head to study him. Her eyes were bright, her mouth lush and moist. The quickness of her breathing was echoed in the rise and fall of her shoulders.

"You're not sure about it," she told him. "I understand. And I don't want to ever force you into something you don't like. But you bought these for me. You knew how much I would love them even though I didn't, that I've never asked this of you. You knew it anyway."

"Yes."

"This, between us. It's not a game," Caite whispered, moving closer. "Is it."

"No, Caite." He kissed her. Hard. Taking it, not asking for it or waiting for permission. His thoughts were rough and tumble, his conflicting desires fighting with each other. He didn't want this to be a game.

But what did he want, exactly?

"Take off your clothes," Caite said in a firm, low voice. She put a hand between them to hold off another kiss.

He could've refused her, but then that was what turned them both on so much, wasn't it? That he should have all the power. Bigger, stronger...her boss, for fuck's sake. But he gave it up to please her, and she took it to please them both.

Jamison loosened his tie and tugged it free. He took off his jacket and laid it over a chair. Then opened his shirt buttons, one by one, adding his shirt to the pile. His cock had begun to strain at his pants, and when he slipped out of them, the bulge in his briefs drew Cait's gaze.

"Hold," she said in that voice, the darker tone that got him rock hard in seconds. "I want to admire you for a minute."

And she did, walking all around him in a circle, occasionally touching him. A light drift of fingers from shoulder to shoulder along his collar bone, then down his center line to the first hint of hair leading into his briefs. Her touch tickled, but aroused.

"So beautiful," she told him.

His first instinct was to bristle. Beautiful was a word for women. But when she stopped in front of him to look up at him, no hint of mockery in her gaze, only appreciation, Jamison relaxed into Caite's adoration.

"Take off the briefs."

He did, slowly, adding a little bump and grind to make her laugh. She did, breathlessly. Her eyes shone.

"Put this on." She handed him the blindfold. He tied it over his eyes.

He stood in front of her naked, cock so hard it tapped his belly when he moved. With the blindfold on, every other sense became slowly heightened. He remembered that first night with her. How she'd urged him to let go, and how, though it went against everything he'd ever done, he had.

"I never thought," Caite breathed into his ear, "how much I needed this until you gave it to me."

The leather was smooth on his wrists. When she

touched his hands, he put them automatically behind him, crossed at the base of his spine. His heart thundered in his ears. His breath grew short. Once he did this, once he gave in to her this way...

Her voice teased his ear again. Her lips brushed it. Her touch, gentle but firm, shackled him. "Oh, Jamison, you have made me so, so happy."

That made it worth it. To be naked and bound in the conference room where he was usually the king, to make her the queen, instead. Whatever she wanted to do, he was willing to let her. When she told him to get on his knees, he did. Because he...

"Are you ok?" Caite's whisper, coming from the side opposite of where she'd been, startled him. "I'm not going to hurt you."

He tensed, swallowing against a dry throat. "I know."

"What are you thinking, sweetheart?"

It was the perfect time to tell her that he wanted to make this something permanent between them. Not an office affair they had to hide. It was the perfect time to tell her that he loved her.

But then the creak of the office door alerted him that they weren't alone.

"Holy shit, sorry," came Tommy's familiar voice. "Sorry, Caite. Shit, I was just driving past and wanted to see if you'd come with us..."

Us. Shit. Jamison was on his feet, unable to tear at the blindfold or do a fucking thing with the cuffs on his wrists. He yanked, feeling the silk cord give, thanking every fucking god that would listen and even the ones that wouldn't that he hadn't bought the ones with metal buckles.

"Get out," Caite said, but it was too late.

"Hey, look at that," came Nellie's voice, full of giggles. Which meant Paxton was right behind her. "Wow!"

"Sorry," Tommy said again, and Jamison wanted to rip the guy to shreds. "Nellie, get the hell out of here, this isn't your business."

Caite's hands were on him, but Jamison shrugged away from her touch, turning, furious and ashamed. He yanked again on the cuffs, hard enough to worry that he might break something in his wrists before he broke the cord. His struggle had loosened them enough, though, so that he could peel one off. He ripped at the blindfold and tossed it down. Breathing hard, feeling sick, he started grabbing at his clothes without looking to see who was still there.

Caite stood alone, looking as disgusted as he felt. She said his name, but he held up a hand to keep her from saying anything else. He pulled on his clothes, not taking the time to be neat or tidy with it, just desperate not to be naked any longer.

One cuff still dangled from his wrist, keeping him from putting his shirt on. He tore it free and tossed it onto the table. Caite stared at it. Slowly, slowly, she bent to pick up the blindfold he'd thrown to the floor.

"Jamison," she said. "They're gone. Don't do this."

Everything he'd given her, everything he'd been willing to give, rose inside him like vomit. He shook his head. "This isn't me. This isn't who I am."

He was ashamed to see tears sliding down her face, but even when she reached for him, he couldn't let her touch him. He stepped back, out of reach. At this rejection, Caite let her hands fall to her sides.

"We don't have to," she whispered. "If you don't want to do that, it's fine, it's all right --"

"But it's what you want, isn't it?" He shouted, voice

hoarse and raw as though he'd been screaming for hours. "It's what gets you off, isn't it?"

"It's what gets you off too," Caite cried, then, softer, "and it's not something shameful. Do you feel ashamed?"

He said nothing, but he didn't have to. She read it all over him. Caite trembled, biting her lower lip, then closing her eyes as more tears spilled down her face.

"Oh," she said in a small, wounded voice. "Well, then."

And after that, nothing more had to be said.

Chapter Twenty

"THREE WEEKS." Elise groaned. "Three immortally long, boring weeks until they'll even consider inducing me. If I have to watch another daytime TV show I'm going to explode with boredom. Though I was thinking about that, Caite, taking on some of those clients. Which, by the way, how's it going with the Treasure House people?"

Caite's attention had been snagged by the sight of Jamison heading down the hall to his office and passing her door, but now she returned her focus to the computer screen. "Oh...really well. We've managed to get their visibility rating up in the past few weeks. There's a big event scheduled for tonight, I'll be covering that."

"Is Jamison going with you?"

Caite paused. Jamison hadn't said more than a few words to her since the afternoon in the conference room. Almost a month ago. He'd spoken of business, when necessary, but any other attempts at getting him to talk to her about what had happened were met with stony silence. They were back to where they been in the beginning. He hated her, she thought, for crossing the line.

"I don't think so."

Elise sighed. She looked better than she had the last time Caite had seen her in the office, but her pregnancy was clearly taking its toll. "How's he doing, by the way?"

Caite didn't answer right away, not sure what her other boss was getting at. "Um, fine?"

"I mean, he's letting you do what you have to do, isn't he? He's not being too overbearing?"

A vision of Jamison on his knees, hands behind him, prick proud and ready for her, dried Caite's throat so much she couldn't answer right away. Elise didn't seem to notice. She shook her head.

"If he is, I can talk to him about it. I have every confidence that you're completely competent, Caite. Or else I wouldn't have hired you." Elise paused to take another deep breath. "God, I never thought I'd miss the days of going to the gym. I feel like such a slug."

"Not much longer now," Caite answered. "Before you know it, you'll have a little bouncing bundle of joy to keep you so busy you'll be wishing you could stay in bed."

Elise smiled. "Yes. I can't wait. This event tonight, it's not the usual Treasure House scene. How'd you score it?"

"Tommy is a big supporter of the charity that's sponsoring the dinner dance. I get the feeling that the other two couldn't give a rat's ass about it, but they're contractually obligated to all go to the same things. He twisted Pax's arm, and of course, whoever Pax goes, Nellie follows. They got matching tattoos last week. Got a surprising amount of negative commentary on it, too." Caite paused, leaning back in her chair so she could casually strain for a glimpse of Jamison's office door. She looked back at her computer to find Elise giving her a quizzical look. "Anyway, this event's a great way to gain some positive spin on the three of them as well as the show. Tommy's donating a huge portion of his Treasure House prize to the foundation."

"If they win it. Well, it will definitely be good publicity and should lead to some other good opportunities, so long as they behave themselves." Elise yawned. "But I guess that's why you'll be there, in case they don't."

"Damage control," Caite murmured. "That's my job. Fixing things when they've gone bad."

The question was, she thought as she and Elise disconnected their call, would she be able to fix what had gone wrong with her and Jamison?

Chapter Twenty-One

IN A ROOM FILLED with the light of hundreds of candles, Caite Fox looked luminous. It was the only way to describe her. And Jamison hated it, because he couldn't stop trying to find her with his gaze, no matter where she went in the room.

Three weeks. Three heinously long, tense weeks, since the nightmare of being found in a compromising position had sent him over the edge. He'd seen her every work day after that, of course, but they'd done little more than send each other memos or have Bobby relay messages. The atmosphere in the office had been...tense. At least for him. Caite hadn't seemed to be bothered much by it at all.

He'd been unable to stop thinking about her. Being underneath her. Pleasing her. For the first time since puberty, when he'd started fantasizing about sex, Jamison's dreams hadn't focused on what he was going to do "to" a woman, but rather what he could do "for" her. And nothing seemed to ease the ache.

"Hey, man." Tommy clapped a hand on Jamison's shoulder. "Thanks for coming out."

The kid had cleaned up pretty good, Jamison noted. Suit, no tie, but his long hair had been tied at the nape of his neck with a cord. A faint pattern of bruising on his cheek made him a little less pretty. Jamison still wanted to match it on the other side with his fists.

Instead, he forced a grin. If the little prick intended on making something out of what he'd seen, he'd have Jamison to answer to, client or not. "Part of my job."

Tommy laughed but like they were buddies, not like he was making fun. "I hope we can count on a donation from you, anyway. At least bid on something from the silent auction."

Jamison turned to look him in the eyes. "This foundation, it means a lot to you."

"I lost my kid sister to Creutzfeldt–Jakob disease. There isn't much known about prion disease. If I can help out, even a little..." Tommy shrugged. The two men stood in awkward silence for a minute before Tommy spoke again. "She's a prize, you know. Caite. She's the kind of woman a man would do anything for. Am I right?"

Jamison's fists clenched, though half-heartedly. The kid was right, after all. "I bet you would."

"Damned right I would. And be glad of the chance to make her my queen...but you know something about that, don't you?" Tommy took a step back as though expecting Jamison to lunge at him. Not like he was scared by the thought. More like he was being cautious.

"Look. I don't give a flying fuck what you think," Jamison began but cut himself off when Tommy held up a hand.

"I get it, man. I get it more than you could possibly imagine. And I envy you. The way she looked at you...I won't lie. I'd give up anything to be able to give it up to her."

Jamison was silent.

Tommy lifted his chin toward the crowd in front of them. "You think any other woman out there can give you what she can? Be the woman you need, deep down in your soul? Because if your answer's anything other than no, I'm going to take her from you. If she'll have me."

For a second or so, it felt as though the floor physically tilted, but it was only his equilibrium. Jamison's lip curled. "You could try, I guess."

"Wouldn't have to try too hard, would I?" Tommy gave Jamison a wicked grin. "Seeing as how you're just standing there, watching her walk away."

In the next moment, Tommy was tugged away by a fawning woman who'd earlier given Jamison his raffle ticket. Jamison watched them go, feeling a lot more respect for the reality star than he had before. With a quick check of the social media stream, reassured that Caite's handiwork of timed updates was doing its job, he headed for the small room off the main banquet hall where the silent auction had been set up. There was the usual--handcrafted baskets filled with soaps or wine or chocolate. Gift certificates to local spas or for holiday home rentals. But there, off to the end, was something he wanted the moment he saw it.

"Pretty, huh," Caite said quietly.

"Gorgeous."

She meant the necklace, a single strand of creamy antique pearls displayed on a velvet mat. He meant her. But he kept his eyes on the necklace and the sign-up sheet. The bidding had already gone over two hundred dollars, still an insanely cheap price for real pearls.

"They're vintage," she said. "Came from an estate. They're not farmed pearls, either, you can see how they're not exactly matched."

He let his gaze drift to her. "You know a lot about pearls."

"Not really. Just what I like." She looked at him, finally, her gaze warm but not intimate.

It pinched at him, the way she let it slide away from him as though he'd never feasted on her pussy and tasted her coming on his tongue. "I'm surprised you don't prefer diamonds."

"Why? Because all women are supposed to like them better?"

"No. Because pearls seem soft."

Her eyebrows rose. "I didn't figure you spent any time at all thinking about what sort of woman I was. At all. Or what I like."

With that, she stalked off, and Jamison watched her go before shaking himself into action. He followed her from the ballroom to snag her elbow, bared by her sleeveless gown. Her skin, warm beneath his fingertips, was smooth as silk. He turned her. He was gripping too hard, he saw when she winced a little and tried to pull away from him. He let her go.

"Caite. I want to talk to you."

He didn't miss the way she looked all around them before meeting his eyes again. "About?"

"Just come with me." Before she could protest, he'd taken her by the elbow again to hustle her down a short hallway used by the waitstaff. By the time they got to a small alcove by the elevators, she'd tugged herself free of him.

She turned to face him. "What's going on? Is it something with the clients? Because Nellie and Paxton have actually been on their best behavior at this thing, and Tommy is..."

"No," Jamison said. "It's not about them. Your handling of things had been...exemplary."

"Ah." She leaned against the wall with her hands flat on it next to her. "So. What, then?"

He kissed her.

Long and hard and fierce, one hand sliding beneath the fall of her sleek blond hair to cup the back of her neck. For a second or so he thought he'd severely misjudged, but when she whimpered into his open mouth and put her arms around him, he bent back to the kiss with added fervor. They ate of each other, mouths and hands and moans all together. When he broke, gasping, to breathe, Caite wound her arms around him and pulled him back in.

"We could do this forever," he said after another few minutes of her mouth making him crazy. "But we should do it somewhere else."

Caite blinked, the haze in her eyes fading. She smiled a little. "Is that what you want?"

"I want you," he said in a low, growling voice he barely recognized. Everything about her made him crazy...no, he thought as she stepped out of his arms to straighten her dress and smooth her hair. To wipe at the corners of her mouth where his kiss had smeared her lipstick. Being without her had made him lose his mind. Being with her again had made him sane.

She looked over his shoulder at the passing waiter heading back toward the ballroom. "I have work to do, Jamison."

"After."

Caite paused, letting her tongue slide over her lower lip. "I don't know."

He took two steps back from her. His fists clenched; she saw it, but didn't look scared. Her gaze flickered. Again, the swipe of her tongue across her lips. The hitch of her breath made him think that while she was playing at being reluctant, she might actually want him, too.

"After the banquet and dancing," she said slowly. "Then we can talk."

He nodded. Neither of them moved. Caite tipped her chin up, her hands flat again on the wall, one on either side of her thighs. She turned her head slowly, slowly, exposing the line of her neck and throat to him. It drew him, moth to flame, bee to flower.

"No," she breathed when he moved closer. "After."

Chapter Twenty-Two

CAITE HAD HEARD the term weak in the knees, but had never understood it until now. She'd waited until Jamison had gone, leaving her near that elevator before she could let out the breath she'd been holding. She'd had to hold onto one of the stacked chairs along the wall and force herself to drag in breath after breath to keep herself from dropping to her hands and knees to stop the world from spinning. It had taken every bit of strength she'd had to keep herself from climbing him like a tree, right then and there.

After, he'd said, and she had agreed.

But what would that mean? After the dinner, which she couldn't bring herself to eat. After the dancing, which had just begun. And then what? What could they possibly have to say to each other, she wondered as she returned to the ballroom.

"Great night." Tommy was well-known for his taciturn nature, but just now he was beaming. He looked around the room, catching sight of Nellie and Paxton holding court, and if it annoyed him, he barely let it show. He put an arm around Caite's shoulders, easing her closer to say into her ear, "Thanks for all your support, Ms. Fox. Without Wolfe and Baron, and really, mostly you, this event wouldn't have had half the attention it's been getting. Online donations have doubled."

"It's a good cause." She slipped an arm around his waist for a second to squeeze him in return.

He looked at her. "The foundation wasn't your client, I was. But even so, you really went above and beyond. I recommended they take a look at hiring you for some future events...it's non-profit, so I'm not sure what their budget is..."

"We do *pro bono* work for a few different places. I'm sure I can work with them." She gave a satisfied sigh, looking around, trying not to act like she was looking for Jamison.

"He's over by the silent auction stuff." Tommy laughed, leaning closer again to whisper into her ear. "But dance with me, first."

She eyed him. "What makes you think I was looking for him?"

"He's the boss, right? Making sure it all goes okay. Boss man." Tommy laughed and shook his head. He offered her his hand.

She took it, letting him lead her to the dance floor, where he settled his hands easily on her hips and led her into a few simple steps. They talked as easily as they danced--Tommy was passionate but also well-educated about the disease for which he'd spent so much effort raising money, and Caite admired both his enthusiasm and his knowledge.

"We're going to start calling out the winners of the silent auction, feel free to keep dancing! Winners, if your name's called, come on up to the front here to get your item." The voice from the front of the room echoed a little through the mic. The silent auction signaled the end of the night.

"You know, there's a lot more to you than meets the eye," she said.

Tommy laughed and spun her slowly out, then in for dip. "I could say that about a lot of people. You, for example."

"Me?" Caite pretended surprise. "Like what?"

But before he could answer, a big male hand came down on his shoulder. "Can I cut in?"

Tommy laughed and nodded, graciously stepping out of the way so Jamison could take his place. When he had, Jamison looked down at Caite with what had become a familiar heat blazing in his eyes. "I didn't like the way he was handling you. You know you don't have to let him, right? Just because he's a client?"

Caite frowned, looking past him to where Tommy was now standing for photos with Nellie and Pax. "It wasn't a hardship, Jamison."

Jamison said nothing in reply. Not with words. His expression said it all, and though she kept hers carefully neutral in response, inside, she warmed. She moved herself a little closer, into his arms, tipping her head back to look at his face.

"You're protective," she murmured.

"I wanted to make sure he wasn't bothering you."

"You wanted to make sure no other man was touching me," Caite said.

She hadn't known for sure it was the truth until she saw his reaction, a thinning of his mouth. Narrowed eyes. And, against the front of her, the sudden press of his erection. She smiled and looked away from him to keep herself from jumping into his arms and feasting on his mouth.

"We can go now," Caite said, already thinking about

the promise of "after" and what it meant. Her nipples went tight. Her pussy clenched. The heat in her stomach kindled higher. Hotter, rising to her throat.

"Not just yet."

Curious, she looked at him, just as the voice that had been calling out the winners' names for the past ten minutes said, very clearly, "Caitlyn Fox! Congratulations, you won the set of antique pearls, generously donated by one of our volunteer coordinators! Please come to the back of the room to get your prize."

Caite shook her head. "I didn't --"

"I did," Jamison said.

Chapter Twenty-Three

THEY WERE GORGEOUS. The most beautiful piece of jewelry Caite had ever owned. The most expensive, too. She'd made no protest at the banquet when Jamison had slipped them around her throat, but here in his apartment, standing in front of him, she couldn't stop herself from being honest.

"You didn't have to do this, Jamison."

"I wanted to," he said, turning with a glass of whiskey in his hand, the bottle in the other.

"You can't...buy me," Caite said.

For a moment, he only stared at her. Then he put the glass down. The bottle. He crossed to her in three long strides and took her by the arms, hard enough to hurt. Her heart lodged in her throat, pounding, and only half in fear.

"Is that what you think I'm trying to do?"

"I don't know what you're trying to do," she told him. "I don't have any idea about you. Who you are. What you want. I thought I did, but I was wrong."

"You weren't wrong," Jamison said, and went silent.

Caite waited for him to speak, but when he didn't, she

sighed and briefly pressed her fingertips to the inside corners of her eyes. For a moment her shoulders slumped as she fought to find the words she wanted--no, needed, to say. She looked up at him at last, desperate to see something in his face that would let her know what he was thinking, what he wanted from her. For them. But all she saw was a faintly neutral expression. Maybe he was waiting, too.

But there was nothing much she could say, other than the truth. "I'll be tendering my resignation on Monday. I've been offered the chance to represent Tommy's foundation on a permanent basis. Media campaign planning. That sort of thing. It's not in violation of my non-compete agreement. I checked with Elise already."

She'd been expecting a few different reactions, but not this one. Jamison growled. Then came at her like...well, like a wolf running down a deer. Except that Caite wasn't running. She stood her ground when he grabbed her. Didn't even tremble when he crushed his lips to hers.

"No," he said against her mouth. "You're too damn good at the business. Wolfe and Baron can't afford to lose you, Caite."

Everything inside her wanted to explode, but she kept herself very, very still. Jamison buried his face against her neck. Holding her. The embrace softened, and finally, she put her arms around him.

"No," he said again.

She pushed him gently until she could look at his face. "Sit."

He did, in the oversized leather armchair in front of the fireplace, but pulled her onto his lap. She didn't protest. She snuggled against him for a moment, listening to the sound of his breathing.

"Elise isn't coming back to work," Jamison said. "She's

decided to stay home, do some consulting for us on a part-time basis. But mostly stay home after the baby's born."

"She didn't say anything about that when I talked to her," Caite began, but Jamison cut in.

"I talked to her. And we agreed that we wanted to ask you to join the company as a partner. Wolfe, Baron and Fox. We were going to talk to you about it together, but..."

Caite laughed without much humor. "I told you, Jamison. You can't buy me."

"This isn't about buying you!" he shouted, then softened his tone immediately. "I'm sorry, Caite, I didn't mean to shout. Please. Listen to me. I don't want you to quit. I don't want you to leave. I don't want you to leave *me*."

Hope, the most dangerous of emotions.

"I want to believe you. But I don't know you," she said finally. "I thought I did, but I don't. At least, you don't seem to want what I can give you."

Jamison shifted her on his lap. "What I want is you. Hell. Quit the business, don't take a partnership. I don't care. Just give me another chance."

She laughed at that and made to get up, but he held onto her just hard enough to change her mind. "You're ashamed of us, Jamison. Of what we do together. And part of me understands that, because it was all new to me, too. But the other part of me doesn't get it, because when I was with you, I never felt like I was crossing a line. I just felt...good. Happy."

"I did too. What can I do to make you believe me?"

Looking into his eyes, believing him was all she wanted to do. "I don't know."

Jamison frowned. They sat together that way for another minute or so, until at last she cuddled against him, tucking her head into the curve of his shoulder. They breathed together, in and out, in perfect sync. She put her hand on his chest to feel the thumping of his heart.

"I was wrong," Jamison said finally. "I was proud and wrong, and yes, I was ashamed. It's hard, you know. To let go. And to have someone see it...I was embarrassed."

"I know." She nuzzled his throat, letting her tongue taste him for a second or so. Underneath her, she felt him stir, and it made her smile despite herself.

He sat back to look at her face. "Can you forgive me?"

"You're not a man who's used to apologizing." She thought on that for a second. "Thank you. And yes. Of course I can forgive you."

"Can you forget, though?" He smiled a little.

"No." Caite shook her head. "I can't do that. But I can look past it. I can let it be unimportant."

Jamison nodded. "If that's the best I can hope for, I'll take it."

"That's not negotiation," Caite said sternly. "You can do better than that."

Then they were laughing together, slow rolling giggles that surged up and out of them both until the air rang with it. And then they were kissing, over and over again. Hands roaming. He was hard and she was straddling him, cupping his face in her hands. How could she ever have thought she wouldn't give him a second chance?

"I want more than four nights a week with you," Jamison said. "In return, I offer breakfast every morning."

"Done. But you have to give me half the closet space," she told him. "And never, ever use my toothpaste. And I will not use your razor for my legs, even if I don't have one."

"Agreed. So...we have a deal?" he asked, giving her a wicked grin. "Do we sign the contract?"

Slowly, Caite rocked against his hardness until his

fingers tightened on her hips and his lips parted. He got that look in his eyes. And then, she said, "Let's just say the negotiations have begun."

Jamison let out a small groan at the press of her against him. "Is this going to be a complicated negotiation?"

"I don't think so," Caite breathed. "I think it's going to be very simple. You do your best to make me happy, and I'll do the same for you."

"I love you," he said. "And I can't promise you I'll always know what to do, but I can promise you I'm always going to give you everything I can."

"I love you too," Caite said. "And I'll take it."

IF YOU LIKED CROSSING THE LINE, YOU MIGHT LIKE
THESE TITLES, TOO…

Each Thursday night Colleen orders a drink at the bar Jesse tends, and every time, he spends the evening noticing everything about her. When a sudden blizzard closes down the streets all around them, it seems only natural for them to spend the night at the place within walking distance of the bar – Colleen's townhouse.

What happens when one night turns into more? Jesse knows that giving her what she wants – what she is too afraid to demand – turns him on as much as it does her. But can he convince Colleen to let him keep proving it to her?

Or will Colleen let her fear stop her from letting go of the past and all that holds her back from taking a chance on the future?

Julia and Graham met a year ago during a work conference, and neither's been able to forget the other since.

When an unexpected delay leaves Julia with a layover in Graham's city, she decides to take a chance and see if what's been building virtually can happen for real.

They only have a few hours…can a short layover turn into something more?

It's not supposed to be love.

Eric has been looking for the right woman – one who will keep him in his place. Lists, tasks, discipline. He wants it all.

Madeline, cut deep by a past love that tore her apart, isn't looking to start something new. Yet when the tall man with shaggy dark hair succumbs to her desires with perfect precision, all at once casual D/S play no longer seems like enough.

Their meeting isn't supposed to lead to anything permanent. They're not supposed to want more than something temporary. They're definitely not supposed to fall head-over-heels for each other.

But they do.

She had never been more beautiful to him than when she was making him hurt.

Corinne was young once. Reese wasn't the first man she ever loved, but he was the first to submit to her. For awhile they had something special, but it ended badly. She's a little older now — and the wealthy businessman who just bought the company she works for bears little

resemblance to the boy from her past. He's commanding, domineering, and seems determined to push her past her limits. In a flash of anger, she falls back into their old pattern—and Reese falls right in with her.

Before she knows it, she's testing him. Then tasting him. Corrine knows she can't afford to get involved again. Her life is complicated enough without throwing in an old romance, no matter how new it feels. Now if only Reese would stop making her feel like the goddess she used to be…and showing her who's been the boss all along.

But if he wants her, he's going to have to beg for it.

About the Author

photo credit: Whitney
Hart Photography

I was born and then I lived a while. Then I did some stuff and other things. Now, I mostly write books. Some of them use a lot of bad words, but most of the other words are okay.

If you liked this book, please tell everyone you love to buy it. If you hated it, please tell everyone you hate to buy it.

Find me here!
www.meganhart.com
readinbed@meganhart.com

facebook.com/READINBED

instagram.com/meganhartwritesbooks

bookbub.com/authors/megan-hart

amazon.com/-/e/B001IGNWW8

goodreads.com/Megan_Hart

threads.com/meganhartwritesbooks